D1146767

Available in June 2008 from Mills & Boon® Intrigue

Eternally

MAUREEN CHILD

MILLS & BOON™
Pure reading pleasure

*All the characters in this book have no existence outside the
imagination of the author, and have no relation whatsoever to anyone
bearing the same name or names. They are not even distantly inspired
by any individual known or unknown to the author, and all the
incidents are pure invention.*

Dear Reader,

Welcome to NOCTURNE.

I am so excited to be a part of this great new series. Being able to let your imagination run riot is a blast for any writer, and I can't tell you how much fun I had creating *Eternally*.

I love the paranormal. The questions that no one has the answers to. I love wondering what lies just on the "other side of the curtain." And isn't it fun to think that perhaps there are other worlds existing within our world that lie just beyond our ability to see?

In *Eternally* you'll meet Kieran MacIntyre, a member of the Guardians. A group of warriors, recruited at the moment of death to become Immortals, they are all that stand between demons and humanity. For centuries they've lived and fought among us while at the same time, they've kept their very existence a secret.

I hope you enjoy reading about Kieran MacIntyre and Julie Carpenter, the one woman who could make immortality worthwhile – if Kieran can keep her alive.

Love,

Maureen

To the real Bob Robison, friend and all-around nice guy who's been bugging me for years to get into one of my books – and to his wife, Marilyn, for being able to survive the craziness with style!

Chapter 1

The body was found sprawled across Nicole Kidman's star on Hollywood Boulevard.

The tourists who'd spent all night partying, stumbled across what was left of Mary Alice Malone and ended their vacation with a whimper.

Sunlight glittered off camera lenses and shone down on the scene with a merciless glare. Pooled beneath the young woman's body, blood, in tiny dark rivers running from opened veins, crept into the gutter. The dead woman's wide blue eyes were frozen open in surprise, staring into the morning sky. Her left breast was gone, excised, as if by a talented yet depraved surgeon and her yellow silk blouse had been deliberately torn and arranged to expose the injury.

Belatedly a blanket was dropped over the body.

But Mary Alice Malone was long past appreciating the privacy.

Ghoulish crowds jostled for position, cameras clicked and the unfortunate tourists wept. Police strung yellow crime scene tape and hid the pity in their eyes.

In L.A., one murder more or less—even one this vicious—hardly merited more than a mention on the local news channels and a small article on page two of the newspapers.

One man took note, though.

One man stood at the edge of the crime scene, letting his gaze sweep over the gathered mob. He knew his quarry was near. He'd recognized the killer's handiwork. He'd chased him before. And won. Now he would be forced to do it again.

And he knew that this murder was only the beginning.

The party was in full swing and Julie Carpenter swiveled on her desk chair to impotently glare at the door separating her suite from the rest of the house. Eardrum-shattering rock music pumped through the place, the bass making the walls tremble like a tired old man looking for a place to lie down.

Her head throbbing and her stomach growling, Julie surrendered to the inevitable. No way was she going to get any work done tonight.

"Thank you, Evan Fairbrook," she muttered and tossed her pen down onto the legal-size pad of paper in front of her. Letting her head fall back, she stared at the ceiling through gritty eyes and called down one more curse onto the head of her ex-husband.

He couldn't be just a liar and a cheat. Oh, no. Wasn't enough just to sleep with her best friend and God knows how many other women in Cleveland. Evan, it turns out, was a *first-class* weasel. Before Julie had caught on, he'd emptied their bank accounts and stolen her car. If she'd had a dog, he would have kicked it.

She couldn't stay in Cleveland. Not with everyone looking at her, whispering about her, wondering how such a bright woman could have been so knuckle-dragging *stupid*. Julie sucked in a gulp of air and reminded herself that moving to California had been a good thing even though she missed her folks and her younger brother. She was in a new city, with a new job, surrounded by people fortunate enough to have never even *heard* of Evan Fairbrook.

No more suburban split level for her, either. Now she shared a historic old house high in the Hollywood Hills with two women who had become good friends. And, she was reinventing her career. The career that had supported Evan while he got his software business up and running.

The same software business that had folded the minute Evan milked all the money out of it and took that plane to Barbados. Julie's only hope now was that he got melanoma from romping around buck naked in the sun with her ex-best friend Carol.

"On his nose," she mused, smiling. "He should get a big, black hairy mole on his nose. Or maybe another body part he's equally fond of. Yeah. And then it should rot and fall off. The body part, not the mole. Slowly."

As curses went, it was one of her better ones, she thought, enjoying the mental image of Evan standing helplessly watching as his prized member swayed, tilted and dropped to the sand. As for Carol, the treacherous witch, it was enough of a curse that she was with Evan in the first place.

Julie blew out a breath and snorted. "Good for me." A year after Evan had screwed her over, she was able to see the humor in the situation. Sort of. Her pride had been dinged a little—okay, crushed, stomped and spit on—but once Evan was gone from her life, she'd been forced to admit that she hadn't really missed him. So what did that say about her?

She shook her head. Man, it was way too late to do any soul searching. Instead she'd eat the last of the Coney Island Waffle Cone ice cream in the freezer. She got up and headed for the door leading from her suite to the hallway connecting it to the kitchen of the huge old house. The mother-in-law suite she occupied in the 1920's Craftsman-style house was way at the back of the building, usually giving her the privacy she preferred.

She'd been lucky to find this place. Number one, she hated apartment living. But more than that, being a freelance writer for the *L.A. Times* meant she needed a home base that was flexible. She did a lot of traveling and having housemates meant she didn't have to worry about her place while she was gone. Plus, she had company when she wanted it and privacy when she didn't.

Eventually, though, she'd like to move to the beach. And she'd take summers off. And do some damn sand frolicking herself.

Her cell phone rang before she could open her door and she checked caller ID before answering. "Hi, Kate."

"Hi." Kate Davies, one of Julie's housemates whispered into the phone, her voice almost lost in the slam of music still pounding through the house. "Hey, what do you want to eat tonight?"

Julie smiled. Living with two women who considered splitting an M&M a walk on the wild side had its fringe benefits. Neither Kate nor their other housemate, Alicia Walker *ever* ate if they could help it. And since they were determined to maintain their chic, skeletal look, whenever they went out on dates—which, let's face it, was a lot more often than Julie did—they brought a doggy bag back for her.

"Where'd he take you tonight?" Julie asked, hoping for a decent steak for once. If Kate or Alicia brought her back one more box of sushi, she'd sprout gills.

"Oh," Kate whispered, "you'd love it. Ruth's Chris. Just breathing in here I think I've gained two pounds."

"Thank God. Meat."

"So, what'll it be? Filet mignon?"

Julie sighed. "I think I just had an orgasm."

Laughter spilled through the phone. "Baked potato or garlic mashed?"

"Please. Garlic mashed. Definitely." Not like she had to watch her breath or anything. "Order the steak rare to allow for heating up later. And if he's willing to spring for dessert, anything chocolate."

"It's been so long since I had chocolate," Kate half moaned.

"Live a little," Julie urged, catching sight of herself in the mirror across the room. Her favorite jeans were so old and faded, they were more thread than fabric. And her T-shirt covered a figure that was more rounded than was fashionable. But then, she wasn't trying to catch a man, was she?

She closed her eyes to her reflected image and concentrated on Kate again. "Eat something you have to chew for a change."

"I've got a shoot tomorrow, Julie. I can't *eat*."

She rolled her eyes. "Right. Sorry. What was I thinking?"

"How's the party?"

"Haven't been out there yet."

Kate sighed. "Live a little," she retorted, throwing Julie's words back at her. "Go. Have a drink. Talk to people. Maybe a *male* people. Person. Whatever."

Julie pushed away from the door, shaking her head. "No, thanks. Been there, survived that."

"You're too young to be a nun."

"And you're too thin to diet."

"Tell you what," Kate said, her whisper hushing through the phone, "you get laid and I'll eat a sandwich."

"A *whole* sandwich?" Julie teased.

"Half," Kate compromised.

"I'll think about it."

"Good." A pause, then, "Oops. Gotta go. He's coming back from the bathroom. See you later."

"Right. Bye." Still smiling, Julie slipped her cell phone into the front pocket of her jeans and opened the door. Instantly music slapped at her. Thundering drums, wailing guitars and the crash of the bass that jolted through the floorboards and up through the soles of her bare feet.

She shook her head, winced and headed down the dark hall. Sounds of the party drew her through the shadows into the kitchen. The lights were on, glancing off the bright yellow walls and white cabinets, searing into Julie's eyeballs like needles. On one side of the room, a man and woman were wrapped around each other as tightly as shrink wrap on a new DVD.

A quick jolt of envy shot through her, but Julie squashed it.

Sex=Bad.

If her hormones hadn't been doing the happy dance when she'd met Evan, none of this would have happened. Celibacy had to be better than letting your desires lead you down roads that only dead-ended.

Deliberately she turned her back on the couple, ignoring completely the muffled sighs and groans. But her insides twitched and a wash of heat ran through her despite all her efforts. To fight the neediness, she grabbed a spoon from the silverware drawer and headed for the one sensual delight that never let a woman down.

She yanked the freezer open and a chill blast of air wrapped itself around her. Snatching up the carton of ice cream, she took a moment to appreciate the fact that because she shared a house with a wannabe actress and a part-time model, the ice cream she bought was *always* in the freezer waiting for her. Smiling, Julie had the lid off and tossed onto the counter even before she swung the freezer door closed again.

"Whoa!" Startled, she took a step back and stared up into pale blue, icy eyes. "Didn't know you were there."

She hadn't even heard the man come into the room. Not a big surprise, though, considering the volume of the music. Although, she admitted silently, there was no way she could have missed this guy any other way. He shifted his cool gaze to the couple across the room from them and his jaw tightened.

Tall, at least six foot four, he had broad shoulders, long legs, night-black hair and sharply chiseled features. He was dressed all in black, from the jeans that hugged his legs to the T-shirt straining across a muscled chest to the three-quarter length coat that hung to the middle of his thighs.

A coat? In summer?

Ah, life in Hollywood, where image was everything.

When he swung those pale eyes back to her, Julie took a deep breath and a big bite of the ice cream. It wasn't enough to cool her off, though. She had a feeling that standing buck naked in a snowstorm wouldn't do it, either.

He frowned at her, then shook his head and glanced back to where the shrink-wrapped couple were practically horizontal on the counter. Before Julie could say anything, the tall, dark stranger was halfway across the room. He grabbed the guy's shoulder and spun him around.

Lover boy didn't much like the interruption. "Dude, what's your problem?"

"Hey," his girlfriend complained as she tugged her tube top back up to cover most of her breasts.

"Leave. Now."

Something in Mr. Tall, Dark and Dangerous's voice must have gotten through. The shorter man grabbed his girlfriend, swung her off the counter and tugged her across the room. Just before he slipped through the swinging door, though, he tossed back one last shot. "You are *so* lucky I don't feel like fighting tonight."

Julie half laughed as they disappeared into the main flow of the party. "You notice he didn't try to threaten you until he was sure he could escape."

"He's here. I know he's here. Somewhere."

"Who? Hell," Julie said, just a little nervous at being alone with a man bristling with a sense of power, "half of Hollywood's here tonight."

"This is your home." His gaze snapped to hers as his voice, deep and low, rumbled as insistently as the bass.

She swallowed. Everything about this man felt just a little over the top. Danger seemed to flash around him in electrical arcs that might as well have been lit by neon. He wasn't the ordinary guest who showed up to these parties. This man was...*different*. "Yeah. Why?"

He moved in closer and Julie felt heat rippling off of him in thick waves. Just watching him walk—long legs, slow, determined strides— was enough to make a woman go all hot and gooey. Not a man for a recently declared celibate to be around for very long. Her knees wobbled unsteadily even as her pulse kicked up into high gear.

It suddenly dawned on her that because of the noise level, if she had to yell for help, it wouldn't do any good. No one would hear her.

"Have you noticed any strangers here?"

"Huh? You mean besides you?" Julie forced

another laugh and took a bigger bite of ice cream, still wildly hoping the frozen treat would cool off the heat building inside. "You're kidding, right?"

She waved her spoon at the closed swinging door separating the kitchen from the living room. "Everyone here is a stranger. Parties are free-for-alls in this town. One person tells someone, who tells someone else who tells someone and—" she paused for yet another bite of ice cream "—you get the picture."

He scowled and his eyes narrowed. "That's what I thought."

Julie took another bite and momentarily savored the swirl of caramel as she studied him. Okay, maybe she wouldn't need help. What she'd need was a cold shower. Every cell in her body was tingling. Those eyes of his were downright hypnotic. She could almost feel herself leaning in toward him and it took everything she had to lean *back* instead.

His gaze swept the kitchen again, as if looking for something he'd missed in his first perusal. Finally, though, those eyes came back to her and she swallowed hard.

Still, he hadn't threatened her and she wasn't

about to let him know she was even the slightest bit worried. She waved her empty spoon at him, sweeping up and down. "You're an actor, right?"

"No."

"Really?" Was it hot in the kitchen? Or was it just her body lighting up like a bonfire? "Because you've got the whole mysterious man of the night thing going and—"

"You should leave, too."

"Excuse me?"

"Leave," he repeated, reaching out to grab her upper arm. "Now."

His hand touched her bare arm and heat sizzled into life between them.

One of them definitely had a fever. She just wasn't sure which one.

He let her go almost instantly, and his eyes narrowed as he watched her. Like he was blaming *her* for that short burst of fire.

Stepping back from him, Julie said, "It's one thing for you to throw Don Juan and the bimbo out, but this is my house." At least one third of it. And right about now, she'd be really happy to see either Alicia or Kate come marching through that door.

The kitchen seemed to be getting smaller. And hotter. "I'm not going anywhere. But I think you should."

Kieran MacIntyre felt the fire still burning his fingertips and a part of him stood back and wondered at it. Through the countless centuries he'd been wandering this earth, he'd never experienced that jolt. He'd known others of his kind who had and in the beginning, he'd even been jealous of it.

But as time passed and the years piled up behind him like dirty beads on a piece of string, he'd learned that he was the lucky one. He had no distractions to keep him from the hunt. He had no other to worry about. He didn't have to concern himself with agonizing over the loss of a Mate when he'd never found one.

Until now.

He'd first become aware of her three months ago when she'd called his home trying to set up an interview with him. Naturally her request was rejected, but he'd looked her up online and had been immediately intrigued. Her photo had haunted him since and he'd made it his business to keep a distant eye on her. Until tonight of course, when he'd been forced to confront her.

Stray curls of dark red hair escaped from the ridiculous ponytail she wore at the top of her head. Her green eyes were huge in a pale face sprinkled with just a few golden freckles. Instinct pushed at him to grab her. Hold her. Tip her head back, taste her neck, feel her pulse pound beneath his mouth. Fill his hands with her breasts and bury himself in her heat.

His body roared with life and a hunger he'd never known before. And he didn't want it. Didn't need it. He'd survived for this long without a Mate and he'd done a hell of a job of it, too. He'd never liked complications. Not in life and certainly not since his death. Easier by far to keep his distance from the mortal world, do his job and then fade from the memory of everyone whose life he'd touched.

Better to be alone.

Count on no one but himself and the other Guardians.

But she smelled sweet. Fresh.

Alive.

The floral shampoo she used clung to her seductively and he wondered if her skin would taste as good as she smelled. Her high, full breasts rose and fell quickly with her agitated breathing and her eyes seemed to get bigger, wider, as she watched him.

Did she sense the connection between them?

Could she have any idea at all about what was to come?

"Who are you?" she asked quietly, her whisper almost swallowed by the noise drifting to them from the adjacent room.

Who was he? An interesting question. Guardian? Warrior? Knight? Too many answers and not enough time.

He took a step closer, and she moved too, backing up until she bumped into the kitchen counter behind her. She jolted in surprise and dropped the carton of ice cream to the floor.

She couldn't know. Couldn't even imagine the world he moved through.

His gaze locked with hers, Kieran moved in even closer, dipping his head, letting her fill him with scents that drugged him, that poured through him like rich wine.

His heartbeat thundered in his chest.

He had no time for this. And yet, he knew he couldn't leave her without one taste. Since he first saw her photo, he'd known this moment would come—now, he wouldn't waste it. Cupping her cheeks between his palms, he took her mouth, intending only a brief, hard kiss that would assuage the sudden, all-encompassing need raging within. But one brush of her lips to his and he was lost.

She sighed into his mouth and her lips opened for him. His tongue swept into her depths and he felt himself drowning in the heat of her. Senses overloading, his body felt engulfed in flames. She sighed again and the soft sound spiraled through him like knives, tearing through a centuries old apathy as if it were fragile silk.

Her breasts pressed to his chest, he felt the thundering beat of her heart as if it were his own. It shuddered through him, pounding in his head, his blood.

She dropped the spoon and it clattered on the tile floor like a warning bell.

Kieran groaned, let her go and reluctantly stepped away, willing his body into quiet. The instinct to take her was strong, nearly overpowering. She trembled, eyes wide, and he wanted to lay her down on the floor and lose himself in the heat of her.

"Wow," she said softly, "you're really good at that."

He rubbed one hand across his mouth and refused to admit he was shaking. He had no time for this. No time to be distracted by something he wasn't going to claim anyway.

He wasn't here for her.

Exactly.

Kieran had followed the scent of his prey to this house. All day, he'd hunted it, always a step or two behind. Tracking the elusive trace energy signature all demons left in their wake. Now, it seemed that Fate had taken a turn in the hunt. Why else would the beast he sought have come here?

To *her* house?

The power of the beast throbbed in the air, its hunger, its desire pulsing wildly and it amazed Kieran anew that the mortals couldn't sense it. Somewhere in this house, the demon moved freely, already on the hunt, deciding who it would kill and when.

And he was the only man who could stop it.

Chapter 2

"You still haven't answered me," she said, voice tight, eyes wide. "Who *are* you?"

"Kieran MacIntyre." His name, nothing else. She didn't need to know more. Hell, she didn't *need* to know his name. He wouldn't be seeing her again if he could help it.

Her eyes went wide and flashed with excitement. "*You're* MacIntyre?"

"Yes."

"The man of mystery?" she continued and he could almost *see* her mind whirling behind her eyes. "The reclusive philanthropist, Kieran MacIntyre? Seriously?"

"And you're Julie Carpenter. A reporter."

Those amazing emerald eyes narrowed briefly. "How do you know that?"

"When you try to arrange interviews," he countered, "do you actually believe you're *not* being checked out in return?"

"Oh." She nodded then said, "Okay then, that makes sense. And here you are. Isn't this a happy coincidence? You, here, I mean. With me." She practically scrubbed her palms together in eagerness.

"I'm not here for an interview."

"Doesn't mean we can't do one."

"Yes," he said shortly. "It does."

There was no time to waste. Not with her. A distraction was something he couldn't afford at the moment. Even one so tempting as she. Hunger raged and warred with the instinctive knowledge that he was wasting time. The hunt was all that mattered. A century and a half ago, he'd found the demon. And he'd done it without having a Mate by his side. Now, he would do it again.

He could hardly look at her, though, without wanting her. Her mouth was red and swollen from the kiss that he was trying to forget. He'd be damned forever if he let his desires make his decisions for him.

Hell, doing just that is what had gotten him killed in the first place.

Bending down, Kieran snatched up the ice cream and the spoon. As he straightened, the edge of his coat slipped back.

"Is that a *sword?*" Her voice yipped on that last word and he saw fear glint in her eyes.

"Bugger." He shot her a quick look, tossed the ice cream and spoon onto the counter, then tugged his coat back into place. "Whatever you're thinking, you're wrong."

"Sure. Of course." She nodded. "Gazillionaire swordsman. No big. Happens every day. In *Bizarro World.*"

He saw her thoughts wheeling through her brain and easily read the agitation in her eyes. Frustration coursed through him. He'd come to this house following a trail—and because he'd worried she might be in danger. Now, she was clearly imagining herself in danger from *him*.

Why the hell had she shown up in his life? This should have been a simple hunt. Locate his prey, incapacitate it, move on.

But nothing was as it should be.

"I don't have time to explain," he muttered and moved away from her. Easier to think if he couldn't inhale her scent.

She practically leaped toward the phone hanging on the wall opposite the refrigerator. With the receiver in her hand and her finger on the number nine, she said, "Make time, sparky. Give me one good reason I shouldn't dial 911."

In one long stride, he was beside her, wrenching the phone from her hand and hanging it up. Damn telephones. Ever since their invention, things had been harder for Kieran and his kind. Too easy for witnesses to call the police—or worse, some tabloid.

"Because," he said, keeping one hand on the phone so she couldn't grab it again, "the police will only confuse things further."

She snorted. "Most criminals would say that."

"I'm not a criminal."

"Most criminals would say *that,* too." She yanked at her hand, trying to get free, which only convinced him to hold her tighter. She winced and said, "So what's your deal? Is the whole philanthropy thing a front? Or maybe you just like to dress up and scare people?"

"Damn it woman…" His fingers coiled tighter around her wrist.

"Let go of me, you psycho."

Fragile bones beneath smooth, hot skin. His thumb moved over her flesh, distracting her momentarily from the fear still dancing in her eyes. Kieran met her gaze and held it, focusing his power on convincing her that she was safe. "You have nothing to fear from me."

Instead of being soothed as he'd expected, the woman glared at his hand, still holding her wrist. At last, he let her go and she rubbed the spot where his fingers had been. Savoring his touch? Or trying to erase it?

"You're carrying a sword and you expect me to take your word for *anything?*" She slipped out from under the close press of his body and took a step or two to one side. "Who carries a *sword,* for God's sake?"

"Don't try to run," he warned softly. "I'll catch you."

She sagged against the counter. "You probably would. Fine. I won't run. Just…get out."

He stared at her. "If you're thinking of writing a story about this—you should know my lawyers will make that impossible."

"You come into my house wearing a sword, breaking my wrist and *you're* gonna sue *me?*"

"I didn't break your wrist," he said and heard the barely banked anger in his own voice.

"Came close."

"Woman," he muttered, wishing he were somewhere fighting a demon to the death. It would have been easier than dealing with her. "There is more going on here than you know."

"I'm getting that," she said, scowling at him.

He watched her, couldn't *stop* watching her if truth be told. Despite her fear of him, she held her ground. She lifted her chin and looked directly into his eyes, with the strength of a warrior. And this Kieran understood. Respected.

For centuries, he'd wandered the earth. He'd seen the worst of humanity and the best. He'd battled demons and men with the same single-minded determination. He'd been with women who quailed at the sight of him yet yearned for the taste of danger to add spice to sex. But never had he met the one woman who could reach him. The one woman who might, if old tales could be believed, be his salvation.

Even the thought of the word choked him. There was no salvation for those like him. The most he could hope for was another battle to follow the last. To move on through the years, untouched by time, able to adjust the memories of those whose lives he brushed up against so that he remained unremembered.

This he knew. This he expected.

She was a surprise.

Her green eyes fixed on him, he could sense her thoughts, the wild clashing of instinct and desire. She trembled and the strength of her need was as powerful as the fear darting through her.

Before he could think better of it, he attempted something he suspected—*hoped*—had no chance of success.

You are safe from me, woman.

She jolted away from the counter and shot him a look that was both intrigued and horrified. "How did you do that? Talk to me in my head? How could I hear you? What's going on?"

Kieran plowed one hand through his hair, scraping his short, neat nails across his scalp, hoping the minor irritation would distract him from the mess this was quickly becoming. She shouldn't have been able to hear him. Shouldn't have reacted at all. The fact that she had, shook him to the core. "I'm telepathic."

"Ah…" She nodded jerkily and inched closer to the swinging door leading into the party, still barreling along at top volume. She slid one hand across the tiles as if to steady her movements. "Well, that explains everything. A *telepathic* swordsman. Fabulous. Lucky me."

"Stop."

She did. As if he'd fired a bullet at her feet.

Going to her, he grabbed her upper arms and pulled her tightly to him. Her breath left her in a rush as her breasts slammed against his chest.

"I'll scream," she warned.

"No, you won't."

"Why wouldn't I?"

"Because you know I won't hurt you."

She took a couple of short breaths and squirmed against him in a way that made him wish for more time. Her hips collided with his need, thick and hard and every twist of movement was glorious torture.

"I don't even know you, why would I trust you?"

"There's no reason you should. But you do." His mind reached for hers and in that tumultuous well of sensation and emotion, he soothed her with gentle whispers.

"Stop doing that," she demanded, but quit

trying to escape his iron grip. "It's creepy having someone else sneaking through my brain."

"I am no happier about it than you."

Questions boiled in his mind and were just as quickly smothered. He had no time for legends. No time to explore the new territory in front of him. Julie Carpenter had no place in his life nor he in hers. She was an accident. A twist of fate, a distraction thrown in front of him to keep him from his prey.

Damned if it wasn't working.

Through the fabric of her shirt, her skin felt soft, pliant. He wanted to drown in the taste of her, take her scent deep inside him. He wanted to lick every inch of her body and when he was finished, he would begin again. He wanted to fill his hands with the weight of her breasts, suckle at her rigid nipples until she was writhing beneath him, begging for the orgasm only he could provide. And when her body trembled on the very brink, he would join his body to hers, filling her with heat, until, together, they were swallowed by the flames.

Still he let her go, pushing her from him, as if needing the distance between them. He hadn't expected her to hear him telepathically. Only a true Mate could do that. Only a woman destined to be at a Guardian's side could be touched by his thoughts. It had been a test he'd thought she would fail. *Hoped* she would fail.

But she hadn't and now Kieran was a man with even more to consider. He took another step back. The cold, solid length of the sword he carried slapped against his side, reminding him all too well of his true purpose here.

Gleefully, eagerly, it wandered the old house.

The music swelled within it, dancing through its veins, pounding in its head. Hunger roared within, demanding release.

So many choices.

It moved through the crowd, unnoticed in the throng, its fingers trailing across lush bodies, its hot breath dusting sweat dampened skin, its hands longing for a blade.

Soon, it thought.

Soon the blood would run, thick and dark.

Soon, the hunt would begin again.

Behind them, the kitchen door slammed open, allowing in a blast of music and the shouted conversations and laughter of the party.

Julie looked past the broad-shouldered man in front of her to the blond woman grinning at her from the doorway.

"Julie! You're with a guy! Yay you!" Instantly she slapped one hand across her mouth and winced. "I said that out loud, didn't I?"

"Oh, yeah," Julie said, her chin hitting her chest. Trust Alicia to come into the room at exactly the wrong moment. Or was it the right moment? Julie wasn't sure anymore.

"Sorry about that," the other woman said with an embarrassed shrug. "Too much wine, I think."

"It's okay." Giving her roommate a wry smile, she realized that she should actually be *relieved* that the smiling blonde had barged in.

So why wasn't she? Good question, she thought and searched for the answer.

A few months ago, she'd tried every trick she knew to get an interview with L.A.'s own mystery gazillionaire. She hadn't been able to worm her way through his guard dogs—lawyers. Now here he was—big as life, a hell of a kisser, and hey, possibly *nuts*—in her very own kitchen. She didn't even know what to think of him. Gorgeous, sure. Lust worthy, without a doubt. But what kind of man carries a sword and tiptoes through other people's minds?

By all rights, she should be terrified just being alone with him. Yet, the only thing she was really worried about here was her virtue—which, let's face it had disappeared a long time ago.

Besides, if Kieran MacIntyre had wanted to kill her, he could have done it when his tongue was down her throat. She shivered at the memory and squelched the desire to do it again. For heaven's sake, what the hell was going on?

"So," Alicia prompted, nodding her head at Kieran as she spoke to Julie, "who's your friend?"

"He's not my friend," Julie countered, glancing from her roommate to Kieran and back again. Only a moment ago, she'd been worried about being alone with him. Now she nearly resented Alicia's presence. "I just met him," she said, avoiding for some reason, giving her friend Kieran's name.

One blond eyebrow lifted and Alicia grinned. "Way to go, Jules."

"Oh, yeah, yay me," Julie muttered, her gaze swinging back to the man in front of her.

Alicia laughed and walked straight to the refrigerator, swaying her hips in a timeless invitation that was more unconscious than deliberate. "See? I've been telling you for weeks that you have to get your head out of your work once in a while."

"Yeah, well…" She glanced at Kieran, but he wasn't looking at her anymore. Instead his ice-blue eyes were locked on her roommate.

Typical.

Well, what did she expect? She wasn't exactly dressed for seduction, that amazing kiss notwithstanding. Then she noticed that Kieran was looking at her again. "She's your friend?"

"Yes," Julie said, glancing now at Alicia, who was rooting around in the fridge. "She lives here with me."

"She should leave," Kieran said softly, his voice somehow carrying over the slam of the party noise.

"Huh?" Julie moved away from him. For God's sake, was the man going to try to empty the house one person at a time?

Alicia hooted, "Hah! I knew there was another bottle in there somewhere!" She dragged her prize, a bottle of chardonnay out of the fridge before shutting the door again. "Who's leaving?"

"Nobody," Julie said, never taking her gaze off Kieran. The man could melt steel with that hot glare, but she wouldn't back off.

Alicia stepped up beside Julie. "He wants us to leave? Our own house?"

"For your safety."

"Uh-huh." Alicia nodded slowly, as if soothing a crabby three-year-old. "Okeydokey. Julie honey, I'm going back into the party now. You coming?"

The overhead light shone down fiercely, throwing Kieran's features into sharp relief. He looked... otherworldly. Mysterious. Dangerous. And just a little bit—okay a *lot*—sexy. Shadows hid his eyes, but Julie felt the power of them just the same.

"Something's wrong here," he finally said, though he looked as though he wanted to say more.

"I'll say," Alicia muttered and gave him one last dismissive glance before turning her attention to Julie. "Come on, Jules. Let's go."

"No," Julie said, still looking at Kieran. She didn't know why, but for some reason, she wasn't ready to walk away from her sword-wielding mystery kisser. "I'll be fine."

Alicia turned a glare of her own on Kieran. "If he bugs you at all, call the cops."

"Don't worry."

"Honey, I never worry," Alicia said with a wink, still ignoring the man watching both of them. "Makes wrinkles."

She never looked at Kieran again when she left the room.

"You won't leave?" he asked when they were alone again.

"No."

He nodded. "I can't promise to protect you."

"Who asked you to?" Her spine stiffened even as a tiny curl of worry unwound in the pit of her stomach.

Funny, but in the six months she'd been in Hollywood, she hadn't felt the need for protection. Until tonight. This moment.

"It's my duty," he said, crossing the room to her in a few long strides.

"You just met me and I'm suddenly your duty?" How she'd managed to speak past the huge knot in the middle of her throat was a mystery. Almost as big a mystery as the man crowding in way too close to her.

He backed her up against the counter until she felt the cold tile pressing into the small of her back. She shivered, but she knew damn well it wasn't the cold causing it. No, it was the *heat* pouring off of him to surround her, to invade her, to make her want...oh, boy.

How was it possible that her normal, everyday life had taken such a completely weird turn in the span of about twenty minutes? And how could she be more interested in feeling him hold her again, kiss her again, than in figuring out what the hell was going on around there?

"You won't leave. I accept that."

"Gee, thanks."

"Stay in your room. Lock the door."

"Trust me," she whispered. "First thing on my agenda."

"I'll be back."

"Great," she said, "movie quotes."

"I don't know what to do about you," he admitted, lifting one hand to trail his fingertips along her cheek, then slowly, softly, down the length of her throat.

Julie sucked in air through gritted teeth and tried to ignore the feeling that her blood was bubbling in her veins. His fingertips strayed to the scoop-neck collar of her shirt and she held a shaky breath, waiting...*hoping* he wouldn't stop. But he did and she wanted to grab at him.

God.

She'd never felt anything like this. Hadn't known she *could* feel this. Sex with Evan hadn't exactly been the stuff romance novels talked about and her one other lover, a guy in college, hadn't been much better. But this guy made her think that maybe there was *more* to discover.

And how crazy was she? Standing in a kitchen fantasizing about a mind-reading gazillionaire with a sword?

He grabbed her when she would have slipped away, then keeping a tight grip on her arm, he lifted his head, closed his eyes and concentrated. Seconds ticked past, marching in time with Julie's heartbeat. She stared up at his face, studying his sharply defined features, noting the strength in his profile.

Finally he opened his eyes and looked at her. "It's gone."

"It?" She shook her head, more confused than ever. "What it?"

"I have to leave."

"Right," she whispered, nodding jerkily. Probably better all the way around if he left. Quickly. "Good idea. You go. I stay. But first tell me what this 'it' is."

"Doesn't matter now. You may be safe, but there's no way to be sure." He stepped back and away from her as if desperate to put a little space between them. His gaze moved over her face with a touch as sure as his fingertips had been only a moment before. "I shouldn't have met you tonight. There's no room in my life for you."

Julie inhaled quickly. "I don't have room for someone like you, either."

"Wanted or not, we *are* connected," he muttered, more to himself than to her. "I don't yet know what it means."

"Be sure to let me know when you find out," she murmured, still shaken.

He stalked to the back door, yanked it open and started outside. Then he paused, caught between the dark and the light and turned to spear her with a hard look. "Lock your door."

When he was gone, Julie slumped against the counter and blindly reached for the now melting carton of ice cream. She lifted it and drank down what she could, before grabbing a fresh spoon and heading for the back door. She turned the dead bolt, hooked the chain and swept the yellow curtain aside to look out into the darkness.

Kieran was already gone.

Swallowed by the shadows.

And standing in the brightly lit kitchen, she felt a tremor of unease slip through her. Throat tight, heart pounding, she headed for the dark hall and her rooms beyond.

With every step, she felt unseen eyes watching her. The fine hairs at the back of her neck lifted and a chill swept along her spine. Her steps quickened, her breath shortened. Fear walked with her when she stepped into her room and slammed the door closed. Leaning against it, she turned the cold, brass dead bolt, then the antique key in the doorknob and waited for her heartbeat to return to normal.

Kieran pulled a satellite phone from the inner pocket of his coat and flipped it open. Stabbing the speed dial, he waited while on the other end of the line, a phone rang and rang. Finally…

"Santos."

"What took you so bloody long?"

A laugh rippled across the line. "Kieran. Should have known I'd be hearing from you. I heard it escaped again."

Kieran scowled, glanced down the darkened street and crossed it hurriedly, moving toward the black Lexus he'd left just beyond the reach of streetlights. "There's been a kill. This morning."

"Didn't take it long."

No, it hadn't. But then, the demon had been locked safely away for more than a hundred years. Of course it would want to revel in a fresh kill right away. The trick would be to keep it from doing any more damage.

Kieran punched a button on his key ring and unlocked the car as he approached. He opened the driver's side door, but before getting in, he paused, concentrating, focusing his energies toward the beast he must find.

"You have its trail?" Santos asked.

"*Had* it," Kieran admitted, glancing back over his shoulder toward the house where he'd left Julie Carpenter. He'd allowed himself to become distracted by her. He'd filled his mind with her scent and forgotten about the other. About his mission. Hard to believe. "Gone again now."

"So you are calling for reinforcements?" The Spaniard's voice was tinged with amusement.

"No," he said, confident in his hunting abilities. He'd never needed help before. He wouldn't this time, either. At least not with the actual hunt. As a Guardian, he'd done his duty over the centuries, accomplished whatever task was set in front of him.

This time, he swore, would be no different.

Even though, it already was.

"Look," he said, taking off his sword and tossing it onto the passenger seat before sliding into the car and buckling his seat belt, "what do you know about Mates?"

A deep chuckle rumbled into Kieran's ear and he glowered even while he fired up the engine and threw the car into gear. "What the bloody hell is so damned funny?"

"Ah, my friend," Santos said, his Castilian accent flavoring every word, "it was only a matter of time before you would come to me with such questions."

The Spaniard's sense of humor could strike at any moment, usually when it was least appreciated. But they'd been friends for five hundred years.

Ever since that night in old Madrid when the two of them had held off a crowd trying to burn another Guardian, Adrienne Marcel, as a witch. Not that the Immortal would have died in the fire, but recovery from severe burns could have taken her years.

Tonight Kieran was in no mood to play games. "Meaning…?"

"Meaning, that an English knight will never be the lover a Spaniard is." He laughed again. "I will be happy to give you any tips you require."

Kieran rolled his eyes, steered his car around a corner and headed down the hill toward Hollywood Boulevard. If nothing else, he'd go back to the scene of the first kill. Look around. Try to pick up the trail again.

"I'm not *English*," he growled, "as I've told you a thousand times and more. I'm a Scot and the day I need help screwing a woman is the day you can bury me."

"Ah," Santos said with only a twinge of regret, "but burial is not for the likes of us, my friend. One only buries the dead, yes?"

"We *are* dead, Santos. We just don't know enough to lie down." He stared at the twin slashes of his headlights, slicing through the darkness, spearing into the bushes and trees crowding the edges of the narrow road. A flash of red eyes as the lights crossed them but Kieran didn't slow. It wasn't the demon. Only another nocturnal animal.

"This is true, Mac. But I think it was not the point of this call to discuss the sad state of our too long lives."

"No." Too long? He didn't know anymore. He looked at mortals and sometimes wondered how they could be satisfied with eighty or so short years. But he'd had centuries to fight and sometimes he thought perhaps the mortals had the better deal.

He took another sharp turn as his thoughts splintered. He glanced at the speedometer and slowed down a fraction. One thing he didn't need was one of L.A.'s finest giving him a ticket. "I want to know what you know about *Mates*. The Guardian legend."

The legend Kieran had never put much stock in, despite the few Guardians he'd known over the years who had actually found women to bind themselves to. Perhaps, then, it wasn't that he couldn't believe in the legend itself, but that it held no truth for *him*.

"Ah." Curiosity colored Santos's voice as he asked, "You have met…"

"A woman."

"Always a good place to start."

"She's…different." Stupid word. Incomplete. Julie Carpenter was more than different. She was a flame to his dry tinder. The heat to his cold. And just thinking of her now tightened his body until the ache of it nagged at him like a rotten tooth.

"What do you wish to know?"

"Everything that isn't common knowledge," Kieran said flatly as the Lexus finally reached the bottom of the hill. He took a hard right, weaving in and out of traffic like a man with a death wish— or a man to whom death meant nothing. "I've never bothered to find out more than the basics before. Now I want to know. So discover whatever you can and get back to me."

"And the beast?"

"I can handle it."

"If you change your mind, I'm near." He paused, took a drink of what Kieran knew was probably Napoleon brandy, "I followed my quarry to San Francisco."

"You get it?"

"Was there any doubt?" Santos chuckled.

"No," Kieran said, smiling now. As a warrior, he could appreciate the talents of another. "I've never known you to fail."

"Nor you, my friend. After all, we have reputations to protect," Santos mused. "Now, I find I am enjoying the view from my hotel of the bridge on the bay. I will be in the city for a while yet."

"Thanks. I'll let you know if I need assistance." He hung up and tossed the phone onto the passenger seat beside him.

Though he wasn't interested in asking for help, Kieran admitted to being glad for the knowledge that Santos was close by. Still, thanks to satellite phones and private jets, no Guardian was isolated anymore.

So many things had changed over the centuries, he thought, drawing to a stop at a red light. His gaze moved over the crowded sidewalks. Hookers, dressed for business, lounged against the sides of buildings and waved desperately at passing drivers. Homeless men and women crouched in dirty doorways and teenagers looking for trouble strutted in packs.

Kieran looked at them all as the beast would.

As potential victims. Wandering from light to shadow, the people moved, separate and apart.

And he realized that no matter how much had changed, death remained the same.

Chapter 3

The crime scene tape was long gone. As a reminder of what had happened, though, dark splotches of dried blood muddied the sidewalk under the pale yellow wash of a nearby street-light.

Nicole Kidman, movie star, had deserved better. But then, so had the young woman whose life had ended on a dirty city street. Moving about the scene, Kieran searched for the faint energy trace left in the wake of all demons. Not much more than a smudge on the air, it was a key weapon in fighting the beasts. But the scent of it had already dissipated enough that tracking in the usual way would be unfeasible.

So, he took a chance.

Kieran stood on the sidewalk star and opened his mind, reaching blindly for a connection to the demon. Not that a telepathic connection was always possible. Every demon was different— though all provided that faint trace element—each of them had different abilities and weaknesses. This particular demon was slightly telepathic— something that just might help Kieran find it.

He frowned as he concentrated. Snatches of malevolence slapped at him, but nothing complete. Nothing substantial enough to help him in his hunt. But the demon was even older than Kieran, so its ability to evade pursuers wasn't really surprising.

Just frustrating.

Disgusted, he scanned the area, discounting the cluster of cars with irate drivers cursing at each other as they sat, locked in congestion. The traffic never changed here. Two in the morning or two in the afternoon, the cars would be stacked up bumper to bumper. Idly he thought that the time of horses had been much better. Though he'd been among the first to buy an automobile, he'd missed the companionship of a horse.

A blond hooker walked slowly past him, shooting him a quick, appraising look, then scurried on, limping slightly on sky-high heels. A young man

with wild eyes and a scraggly beard handed out
flyers inviting passersby to one free drink at a local
topless bar and the neon sign across the street from
Kieran fluttered like a racing heartbeat.

The demon could be anywhere by now. Could
have even left the city in an attempt to escape *him*.
But Kieran didn't think so.

This particular demon was a creature of habit. It
preferred crowded areas, where people were practically stacked on top of one another. And usually,
when it found a place, it locked in on it. The last
time, in 1888, it had been London, the East End.

Whitechapel. A section of the city so crowded
with back alleys and a twisting, sinuous layout of
tenements and bolt holes that it had taken Kieran
almost five months to track it down.

Just thinking about that time, brought it all back
with a rush that filled his mind. The damp fog
swirling through filthy, overcrowded streets like
gnarled fingers of smoke, coiling around the
unwary, holding them fast in the bowels of the
city. He could almost smell the greasy stench of
bad liquor and the nearby slaughterhouse. The
layer of hopelessness and decay that had colored
every square foot of Spitalfields.

Five long months he'd spent in that miserable hellhole. He'd tracked the demon relentlessly—not an easy task since the damned thing had changed bodies too damned often. But Kieran had finally caught the vicious bastard. Just like he would this time.

Turning abruptly, Kieran started down Hollywood Boulevard. Even late at night, the sidewalks were crowded. Not so much with the tourists, who usually had enough sense to keep to their hotels, but with the local denizens who reclaimed the street every night.

Teenage runaways, caution in their eyes, grouping together for whatever protection they could find. Homeless men digging for food in trash cans, and the ever present hookers, masking their own fatigue with brittle smiles and half-hearted come-ons.

Here on the streets, no one expected anything from him. No one knew he was actually Kieran MacIntyre, wealthy man with a mysterious background. Here, he was simply known as "Mac." A solitary man with a hard eye and little patience. Kieran blended into the background, becoming a part of those who wandered in the darkness.

Women watched him as he passed and, mostly, other men steered a wide path around him.

"Hey, Mac."

He stopped, looked to the right and nodded at Howie Jenkins. A Gulf War vet, he kept his Purple Heart proudly attached to a stained gray overcoat he wore religiously, winter and summer. His salt-and-pepper beard hung to his narrow chest, and his blue eyes were filmy with an alcoholic haze.

But despite what his life had come to, Howie still had a soldier's soul. Making him an excellent fount of information from time to time.

"Howie. How is everything tonight?"

"You know," the man said, keeping one fist tight on the shopping cart loaded with his worldly belongings. "Same ol', same ol'."

"Have you seen anyone new lately?"

Howie laughed, a raw, grating sound that rattled in his chest until he coughed hard enough to hack up a lung. When he finally caught his breath, twin flags of bright red shone on his sunken cheeks. "That's a good one, Mac. Hell, there's always somebody new around here. Don't always last, but they always come."

"True enough," Kieran muttered, letting his narrowed gaze sweep the street again before shifting back to Howie. "This one would be different, though. He'd stick to the shadows. Watching women."

There was no way to know what this demon would look like now. It could manifest in this dimension, but mostly, it chose to inhabit the body of a willing mortal. And God knew there were plenty of evil souls in L.A. for the demon to choose from. As in Whitechapel, the demon could slide from body to body, always changing its shape and appearance in an attempt to elude the Guardian assigned to track it.

One thing would not change, however—this demon's lust for blood and its preference for killing women.

Howie laughed again until he wheezed. "Well, we all watch the women, man."

"Not like him."

Something quick and intelligent flashed in Howie's rheumy eyes briefly. Lips tight, he asked, "He the one got that little girl early this morning?"

"That's him."

"We know what he looks like?"

"No." Damn it. The demon could be anyone. It took on and cast off identities with every kill. That's why there'd been so many different "eye witness" reports on Jack the Ripper. Some had seen an older man, tall. Others swore he was a short man of not more than thirty. Scotland Yard had discounted *all* of them. Only Kieran had known that every witness was telling the absolute truth.

Idly pushing and pulling his shopping cart, Howie turned a look on the street and frowned when one of the hookers draped herself over the opened window of an SUV. He nodded in her direction. "Girls like Heather there, ought to be warned."

"You can try," Kieran muttered, knowing that warnings were never taken seriously. Even those who should know better were always convinced that *nothing* would happen to them. Hell, he'd done his best to convince Julie Carpenter that she might be in danger and all he'd accomplished was making her scared of *him*.

Not that he gave a good damn, he assured himself.

Still, thoughts of her brought a buzz to his veins and an ache to his groin. In those few stolen moments, she'd gotten to him. A couple of kisses, a quick grope, and those big green eyes and she'd infiltrated his mind.

"Nah," Howie was saying now as Heather climbed into the car with her latest customer. "They won't listen."

"Probably not."

"You're huntin' this guy?"

"Yeah," Kieran said softly. "I am."

"Then you'll get 'im."

He would. But in Whitechapel, five women had had to die miserable deaths before Kieran had caught up to the demon. And if it hadn't enjoyed itself so much with its last victim, Mary Kelly, giving Kieran enough time to track the scent of blood and fear…

"Keep your eyes open for me," he said abruptly and reached into his pocket for the wad of bills he kept ready. Peeling off a fifty, he handed it over and watched it disappear in a wink into Howie's coat pocket. "If you see something, contact me."

"Always do, Mac," the older man said, already starting down the street, looking for cans and bottles, "always do."

Kieran watched him go, thinking briefly of all the old soldiers he'd known over the centuries. No matter their circumstance, there was always a core of steel to be counted on. And for this hunt, he would need all the steel he could find.

It felt the Guardian's frustration. His anger. And it smiled.

A dark, gleeful joy rose up inside it and the demon held it close, savoring the rush of anticipation. The world had changed much in the last century. Though some things remained the same. It lifted its hands and idly studied them. This mortal it inhabited was young. Strong. The man's soul had been as dark as any it had ever encountered and the demon smiled. It was always so easy to find a willing partner.

Swallowing the mortal's will was simple enough. And so would learning anew how to become a part of humanity. Mortals had advanced much in the last century, but the hungers were still there. And it would feed on those hungers until the city itself wept for mercy.

The beast would slide into the shadows that reached out for the unwary. Become a part of that darkness. It would learn. And kill. And this time, it would not be stopped.

This time, it would defeat the Guardian sent to cage it once more.

Wondrous, to be matching wits with its enemy again. Satisfying to know it had already outmaneuvered MacIntyre. It had left the party earlier, just long enough to lead the Guardian away from the selected prey.

And while MacIntyre roamed the streets, the demon returned to the bright lights and the pulsing music.

To the woman who would die before sunrise.

Julie sat up all night.

Kieran MacIntyre, rich, gorgeous...*crazy* wouldn't leave her mind. Thoughts of him kept stirring up feelings she really didn't want to examine too closely even while her brain kept trying to warn her off. A gazillionaire recluse who came with his own sword?

Just didn't make sense. A few months ago, she'd dug into MacIntyre's life, learning as much about him as she could before beginning her efforts at gaining an interview with him. And nowhere in any of her research had anyone mentioned that the great man himself might just be a real wacko.

"You'd think that would have been worthy of

at least a footnote or two," she muttered, gaze darting around her room—every light she had was on and blazing, chasing off any hint of a shadow. "But apparently not."

No mention of craziness. She frowned, remembering that in all her research there really hadn't been much of anything mentioned. No one seemed to know much about the man who lived in a veritable fortress high in the Hollywood Hills. Oh, there was plenty of information about the charities he'd supported over the years. About the endowments he'd made to inner city foundations and women's shelters.

But there'd been nothing on his background. Who he really was. Where he'd come from. He'd only been in L.A. for ten years, and yet, nowhere was there a note of where he'd been before coming to California.

Why?

Had all previous reporters been too afraid of him to dig too deeply?

Remembering the flash of something dangerous in his icy-blue eyes, Julie could understand that. But at the same time, she had to wonder how Kieran MacIntyre had managed to intimidate all the press.

Frowning, she thought of the sword he kept at his side and realized that maybe it wasn't all intimidation. Maybe he just dispensed with reporters who got too close or weren't scared enough to back off.

"Oh, that's a lovely thought," she mumbled, shaken.

Her eyes felt gritty, her stomach was twisted into knots and her brain hadn't stopped racing all night. Arms wrapped around her up-drawn knees, she heard Kieran's voice over and over again in her mind. She saw his eyes, those pale blue depths that seemed to stare right through her. And she tasted his kiss on her lips.

Everything he'd said replayed over and over again in her mind. Fear warred with desire and lost miserably. She had no proof he was dangerous. After all, he hadn't killed her. And he'd had plenty of time to.

"Great," she whispered. "Just the quality a woman should look for in a man. *'Hey, he hasn't killed me yet.'* Yeah. My hero."

Outside her room, the night crawled past. The party carried on for hours, music, laughter and shouts subtly invading her room at the back of the house. And despite being irritated by the rumble of sound, she was also grateful for it. At least she didn't have to be alone in a silent house with nothing but her own crazed thoughts for company. At least she knew there were other people nearby.

And when the party finally ended, she knew that Alicia and Katie were there in the house with her. She wasn't alone.

Staring blankly while her mind raced, she waited hours for the dawn to streak the sky outside her window. Rocking in place, she watched the night slowly, inevitably, fade. And when those first pale colors deepened into scarlet and violet, she drew her first easy breath.

"Idiot," she muttered, safe now in daylight, apart from the intangible fears that had clawed at her for hours. She crawled stiffly out of bed, and switched off the bedside lamp and the overhead light that had burned throughout the long night.

She'd spent the night terrified—all because of a great kisser with a hell of an act and a sword he probably carried for compensation. He'd scared her, given her dire warnings and despite all of that, nothing had happened.

She hadn't been threatened.

She'd simply been had.

"Does he just enjoy playing night marauder? Suckering some idiot woman into buying that *man of the night* routine?" She pushed her hair out of her face, letting her temper kick in—being mad, much better than being scared. "Does he get his jollies by scaring somebody then disappearing?"

Julie's voice echoed hollowly in her room and didn't give her an ounce of satisfaction. Because despite the fact that nothing had happened to her, that she felt like an idiot for locking herself up and staying awake all night—a part of her still believed that Kieran hadn't been playing games.

"Which means what exactly?" Frowning, she muttered an answer to her own question. "It means that you're talking to yourself. Not a good sign. If you don't watch it, girl, you'll be as crazy as he is."

Groaning slightly as her cramped muscles screamed in silent protest, she stretched, wincing, then stumbled toward the bathroom. As the day began, she stood under a steaming hot shower, hoping the stinging spray would wash what was left of her fears away.

But even as she dried off and smoothed on the jasmine-scented body lotion she habitually splurged on, Kieran's face drifted through her mind again. She closed her eyes and felt his hands on her arms, his mouth on hers, the hard ridges and planes of his body pressed against hers. And something inside her quickened into an eager gallop. Obviously it had been *way* too long.

"Oh for God's sake."

Grumbling, she pushed his memory away, determined to not let him influence her day as he had her night. Fear had kept her company for hours. She'd jolted at every sound, kept her gaze fixed on her locked door and hadn't even relaxed when the party finally wound down and the house settled into silence.

Now she had to get dressed, drop in at the paper and pick up the notes in her desk. She had an interview scheduled with Selene—no last name—hairdresser to the stars. Making a face, she shook her head and reminded herself that these fluff pieces paid well and were usually picked up by the AP.

Didn't take her long to climb into what she privately thought of as her "uniform." Black pants, white shirt, black jacket and black boots. Not exactly a fashion plate, but the photographer assigned to her wouldn't be taking shots of her.

Julie gathered up her briefcase, made sure she had her mini tape recorder, a fresh steno pad and at least three pens with her. Then she swallowed the last vestiges of her nighttime nerves, stepped out of her room and closed the door behind her.

Her boot heels clicked musically on the floor as she walked into the kitchen and stopped dead. It looked like a small nuke had been detonated nearby. Dirty glasses, empty food platters and wadded up napkins littered the counter. A shattered wineglass was splintered across the floor and a curtain rod hung drunkenly from only one hook.

"What the hell?" She took a step, listened to the crunch of glass beneath her foot and winced, stepping wide of the mess and walking along the edge of the room toward the swinging doors.

She pushed the door into the living room open wide and expelled one long, disgusted sigh. The damage in here was even worse than the kitchen. Remnants of what must have been a beaut of a party were scattered throughout the living room and connected dining room. Sofa cushions were half on the hardwood floor, someone's discarded shirt draped across the coffee table, empty arms hanging over the edge and a bowl of chips lay on its side, its contents spread out and crushed into oily oblivion.

Stale cigarette smoke hung like blue fog in the room and the smell fought for precedence over the stink of spilled liquor. Only a few minutes ago, she'd been grateful for her housemates. Now she wanted to kick both of them.

Shaking her head, Julie shoved empty glasses aside and laid her briefcase onto the dining room table. She crossed the room, opened up two of the windows and then, still muttering dire threats, walked into the living room, and stomped across the littered floor to the French doors leading to a tiny, walled patio.

"God, Alicia," she muttered darkly, as her right foot slipped in a puddle of congealing guacamole, "couldn't you at least have picked up the garbage before crashing?"

But, knowing her housemate, Julie figured Alicia had hooked up with some guy at the party and decided to put off clearing the rubble for as long as possible. Alicia wasn't exactly known as

Ms. Clean. And Katie wasn't much better, though she would at least feel guilty for leaving the mess.

Julie turned the latch on the brass doorknob, flung open the French doors to air the house out and took a deep breath of fresh morning air. Irritation simmered inside as she noticed Alicia, stretched out on one of the two cushioned chaise lounges, her face turned away from the house and toward the rising sun.

Still wearing her party clothes, right down to the ridiculously high heels she'd spent a fortune on, she'd obviously stretched out to relax the night before and had fallen asleep.

Shaking her head, Julie started across the flagstone patio and accidentally kicked an empty beer bottle, sending it skittering across the stone and into the bushes lining the wall. She sighed as it clinked against the bricks.

"Alicia," she started, frowning at a swarm of ants climbing a tiny mountain of dried onion dip splattered on the patio. The last of her fear drained away under a rising tide of disgust. "Damn it, Alicia, the house is a wreck and I'm not cleaning it this time."

Usually straightening up after parties fell to

Julie simply because *she* was the only one who couldn't live with the mess. Kate and Alicia's slob tolerance level was way higher than her own.

Still Alicia hadn't moved. Hell, she didn't even stir and Julie's temper spiked up a notch or two. "Hello?" she snapped. "Don't you have an audition this morning?"

Her friend didn't even flinch.

"God." Julie blew out a breath, came up behind the other woman and reaching down, grabbed Alicia's shoulder and gave her a shake. "You could sleep through a bomb blast, couldn't you?"

Alicia slowly tipped to one side, her blond hair falling in a sleek arc, sliding down until her head hung over the edge of the chaise. A bloody mockery of a smile ringed the base of her neck.

Julie took an instinctive step back as she stared into her housemate's wide, staring, *empty* eyes.

The bright, cheerful sunlight showcased the river of blood that had soaked into the blue flowered cushion beneath Alicia's body. Birds screeched and tittered from the trees. A car whizzed down the street, its engine roaring.

And on the tiny patio, shielded from its neighbors, Julie felt the world tilt out from under her feet. She took a breath and released it in a scream.

She was still screaming when the first squad car arrived.

Chapter 4

She couldn't stop shaking.

Julie hugged herself tight and hunched deeper into the cushions of the couch. Reaching out with one hand, she pushed a bag of chips out of her way and curled her legs up beneath her. In one corner of her mind, she realized that she was trying to be invisible. To hide from the reality of what her world had suddenly become.

And she didn't care.

God, she wanted out of this house. Away from the scents of blood and the overpoweringly strong mingled scents of aftershave coming from the dozen or so men wandering through her house.

Blindly she stared at them all as if she still couldn't believe they were there. Crime scene investigators jostled uniformed police officers. Radios crackled and whispered conversations rose and fell like the tide as two detectives studied the patio where Alicia still lay as if waiting for evidence to jump up and shout *Here I am!*

Outside the French doors, shade dappled the patio that Julie would never again be able to step onto without seeing Alicia lying there staring sightlessly. A soft wind rippled through the house, caressed Julie's skin and made her shiver.

Crime scene techs twirled their brushes, decorating every flat surface with the graphite powder they used to lift fingerprints. A pointless exercise, since half of Hollywood had been in the house last night. But there were routines to follow, rules to obey and she was too stricken to care what they did.

What did any of it matter now?

Alicia was gone and Kate…

The rattle of wheels and metal jolted through the house and she jumped in reaction. Pushing off the couch, Julie ignored every other person in the room and started toward the gurney two men were pushing toward the front door.

"Kate," she whispered, reaching out for her friend's hand and stopping short of touching her. Kate's features were still, her chocolate colored skin seeming somehow pale.

A brilliant white bandage wrapped her throat and IV needles jutted from her arms, trailing tubes hooked to plastic packages dripping fluids into her body. Julie's stomach lurched and tears she'd thought dried up stung her eyes again. Even breathing hurt, as if her lungs were being squeezed in a vise.

How could this have happened?

How could Alicia be dead?

How could Kate be so badly hurt?

What was happening?

"Excuse me, miss," one of the paramedics said brusquely with a quick glance at his patient. "You have to step back, let us get her to the hospital."

"I should go with her," Julie said, staring at Kate's face, unsuccessfully willing her to open her big brown eyes.

"Sorry, not possible." He didn't sound sorry, just hurried. Julie jumped back as they pushed the gurney past her. All she could do was stand there and watch.

Just an hour ago, she'd found Alicia's…*body* and hurried into the house to call the police. That's when she'd found Kate, her other housemate, lying on the floor behind the couch. The same dark red ring circled the base of Kate's neck, but the slice hadn't been deep enough to kill her. Instead Kate was gravely injured, but still breathing. *Thank you, God.*

So far, the police were speculating that Kate had surprised Alicia's killer and in his haste to escape, the killer hadn't taken the time to make sure his second victim was dead.

A sloppy killer.

Should that make her less scared or more so?

God, she didn't know what to do.

Mouth dry, eyes streaming, she turned in a slow circle, trying to get a grip on what was happening. But how could she? No one was ever prepared for this kind of thing. Murders didn't happen in your own home. They happened to some poor slob who was safely distanced from you on the TV set. Killers didn't slip through your house, killing people you loved, leaving them lying in their own blood like forgotten dolls.

Outside the house, media vans were already parked. Didn't take long for news to travel. Not when every television station and newspaper in town was hooked into the police radio frequency. For now, all of the reporters were being stalled at the base of the driveway, held back not by their own moral codes, but by the string of police officers standing guard.

In a few hours, there would be no one to keep them at bay. And she knew her fellow reporters well enough to know that they wouldn't give her a moment's peace. But what could she tell them? That she had one dead friend, one injured friend and that she had no idea why *she* had survived unscathed?

They wouldn't accept that. Hell, she was having a hard time accepting it herself.

Because she had a very good idea why she'd escaped injury.

Not for the first time since this awful morning had dawned, she thought of Kieran MacIntyre. Only the night before, he'd stood in her kitchen and warned her that she was in danger. Told her to lock her door. To protect herself.

How had he known?

And if *she* had been the one in danger, why was Alicia the one who was dead? Why was Kate on her way to a hospital?

And would things have been different if she'd told Alicia about Kieran's warning? Would it have mattered at all? Those questions would be haunting her for a long time to come.

"All clear here," a deep voice said from the patio and Julie spun around to stare through the open French doors.

Two men wearing uniforms that read Medical Examiner, gently lifted Alicia's body and Julie had to close her eyes. Just like every other American with a television set, she knew all too well what was coming next.

The somber-eyed men would lift Alicia's body, lay her down on a sheet of heavy black plastic and then they would zip that body bag closed. Alicia would then be taken to a morgue and closed up in a refrigerated drawer. And she would be no more than a numbered statistic in a town where violent death was the norm, not the exception.

"Ms. Carpenter?"

"Yes." She opened her eyes and looked up—way up—at Detective Coleman. At least six foot five, he had thick black hair, sharp brown eyes and a permanent frown etched into his fortyish features.

He closed his notebook and tucked it into the inside pocket of his jacket. "We've finished here for the time being." Glancing around at the crime scene techs, he added, "They're still processing the scene, and I don't think it's a good idea for you to stay here."

"No, I don't think so, either." She shivered again and folded her arms around her waist. She didn't want to be here.

"One of the officers can take you to a hotel," he offered.

"No." Shaking her head she added, "Thanks, but no. I'm not sure where I'm going yet and…"

"It's okay," he said, not unkindly. "I understand. This is a hard thing." He took a business card from his wallet and handed it over. "This is my number. If you think of anything else, call me. Once you know where you're going to be, call me. I'll stay in touch."

She stared at the card, barely seeing it through the haze of tears still blurring her vision. "Thank you."

When he walked away, Julie simply stood there for a long minute or two. She felt lost. Scared.

Alone.

Kieran only half listened to the police officers moving around the small patio. He wasn't interested in their speculation. He didn't need to guess what kind of monster had killed Julie Carpenter's friend and grievously wounded another.

He already had the answer to that question.

Guilt pinged inside him like an unfamiliar echo and he fought to ignore it. Centuries he'd lived, moving through the mortal world like a shadow. He did his job and never indulged in futile, self-serving waves of guilt for not being able to save the victims who fell beneath a demon's glee. He wasn't the savior of the universe. He was only a warrior. He could only track and kill a demon after it had made its first move.

He couldn't save those who were destined to die.

Irritably he reminded himself that he'd warned Julie of the dangers lurking near her. He'd followed the demon's scent half the night. He'd had no way of knowing the damn thing would double back and make its kill in this house.

But, if he hadn't been distracted by Julie in the first place, he might have caught the demon before it had a chance to kill again. If he'd been doing his job instead of kissing a woman he had no business being around, there might have been two fewer victims.

"Vicious bastard," one of the cops muttered and Kieran had to agree.

And the demon was just getting started.

He walked past the officer, now bent double to search the flagstone patio for evidence he wouldn't find. The cop never noticed him. Guardians had the ability to obfuscate themselves at will, becoming no more substantial than the shadows that crouched on the edges of sunlight.

Stepping into the house, Kieran let his gaze sweep the room, looking past the crime scene people as he searched for the woman who had survived.

Why?

Why had she lived? Had the demon been so bent on enjoying itself with its first victim it hadn't even bothered to look for more?

Movement at the corner of his eye caught his attention and Kieran turned his head to see Julie taking small, uneven steps toward the kitchen. Instinctively he followed her, while maintaining the aura that kept him from being seen.

He kept pace with her through the kitchen and down the long hall that led to what he assumed would be her bedroom. He heard the soft hitch of her breath as her stifled sobs shuddered through her and a long dormant corner of his heart ached to comfort her.

But what comfort was there to offer?

She slipped into her room and closed the door with a quiet snick of sound. Sunlight poured in through a window where the drapes had been tossed open wide. He glanced around her room, then focused on her again as she folded in on herself, dropping to the edge of her bed and covering her face in her hands.

Pain, as unfamiliar to Kieran as guilt, washed over him in thick, black waves. He hadn't even attempted to comfort a living soul in centuries. No doubt he would be terrible at it, so he didn't even try. "Julie."

Her head whipped up and tear-filled green eyes fixed on his face. Shock rippled across her features for a blinding half second and then fury took its place. Leaping off the bed, she charged him. Hands flailing, she slapped and clawed at him in a fit of panic and hurt and anger. Those eyes of hers flashed as she whispered brokenly, "It's your fault. You did this. You brought this here."

He caught her hands in his and held them in tight fists. Kieran felt her pain as surely as if it were his own. The *connection* between them hummed in the air, drawing him in even as he fought the urge to step back and away from her.

"Stop this," he ordered. "It's not helping."

"Helping?" Julie struggled in his grip, yanking and pulling at her hands until finally he released her, more for his own peace of mind than hers.

"Nothing can help," she said hotly. "Don't you understand? Alicia's *dead*. Kate's in the hospital and the paramedics looked as though they were already burying her while they were pumping medication into her body."

"I know," he said.

"You know." She nodded and paced in short, staccato steps, back and forth across her room, pausing only long enough to glare at him. "Of course you know. You told me last night that something was here. Something dangerous." She stopped short in front of him, whipped her hair out of her eyes and narrowed them in suspicion. "How do I know it wasn't *you*? How do I know you didn't attack them?"

Irritated again, with both her and himself, he pushed one hand through his hair and snapped, "You know. You feel it."

"What I *feel*," she countered, suddenly rubbing her hands up and down her arms, "is sick and scared and—Oh God. Alicia's dead."

Her fury was easier to deal with than her misery. Kieran blew out a breath, gritted his teeth and said, "You can't stay here."

"I know that. Don't you think I know that?" She turned away from him, walked to the window and stared out at the tree just beyond the glass. Sunlight shone around her as if she'd been dipped in gold. "I'll never be able to stay here again. I couldn't. Couldn't be here and not see…" She drew a shaky breath and shook her head. "Even if I could, the cops want me out of here. They're sealing the house for the investigation."

"They won't find anything."

She turned her head and the sunlight illuminated one half of her face, leaving the other in shadow. "How do you know?"

"Because I know what killed your friend."

She took a step toward him then stopped. "If you know who did this, you have to tell the police."

"I said *what*," he corrected. "Not *who*."

"What're you talking about?"

"Nothing." He shouldn't have said anything. She wouldn't believe him and it would only make things harder than they already were. "Get your things. I'm taking you to my house. You'll be safe there."

"You're not taking me anywhere." She lifted her chin, stiffened her spine and gave him a look that probably quelled any mortal male she wanted to freeze out.

Didn't bother him a bit.

Ignoring her, he walked to the closet, threw open the door and grabbed an armful of clothing, not giving a damn what he took.

"Stop!" Her voice lifting, she rushed at him again, pulling her clothes out of his grip. Bracing herself in front of her open closet like a castle guard standing between her queen and an enemy. "Just, get out. Get out now. I'm not going any-where with you."

"I can't leave you on your own."

She shot him another death glare. "I don't remember giving you a vote. I'm going to a hotel." She stepped past him to toss her clothes onto the bed.

"Damn you, woman, do you think this is over?" Kieran grabbed her arm and spun her around to face him. He yanked her close until she was forced to tip her head back to stare up at him. When he gave her a hard shake, the topknot her hair was in tumbled loose and her dark red hair fell around her shoulders.

Despite the sense of urgency clawing at his insides, Kieran felt the sharp stab of desire. The need to take her, taste her. To feed the connection between them. To see for himself if all the old Guardian legends about Mates were real.

His fingers on her arms tightened. Her gaze met his and just for an instant, Kieran forgot about his demon prey. Just for an instant, he lost himself in her eyes, and a part of him responded even more strongly to the fury glinting up at him.

"I have no time for you," he muttered, his gaze moving over her face.

"Then let me go," she demanded and gave his chest an ineffectual shove with both hands.

"No."

Lifting her to him, he covered her mouth with his, his own frustration and fury feeding the kiss until he felt as though he were drowning in the taste of her.

Threads of something strong, something ethereal whipped from her to him and back again, stringing them together, binding them in a moment torn from time itself.

The world dropped away.

He held her closer, taking her mouth in a kiss that dragged him to the edge of an abyss he hadn't even been aware of. Her breath mingled with his and Kieran felt the pounding of her heart thrum through his system like a chorus of drumbeats. Releasing her only long enough to scoop his hands up and into the mass of her hair, he took her harder, stronger, needing more.

His tongue caressed hers, his mouth devoured hers. She shifted in his grasp, instinctively moving closer, burrowing into him, surrendering herself with an eagerness that stole his breath.

Julie's body lit up inside with the crashing burn of a sky full of fireworks. From the top of her head to her toes, her skin tingled and buzzed. His mouth on hers was both torment and delight. She knew damn well she should be shoving him away. She didn't know him. Didn't know anything about him except for the fact that he had been there in her house the night Alicia was killed. That he'd warned her of danger.

For all she knew *he* was the source of the danger.

Sanity would demand that she keep clear of

him. But who needed sanity when she could experience the amazing sensations flashing through her body?

Her breasts pressed to his chest and her nipples felt like pinpoints of flame. She ached to have him touch her. To feel his hands on her skin. To see how big these feelings could be.

He groaned and caught her up tightly to him, his arms coming around her like a vise. And her mind suddenly raced with thoughts that weren't her own. As he dazzled her senses with a hunger she'd never known before, she tried to understand the images that rose up in her mind with such rapid intensity she could hardly separate one from another.

Castles, standing proud on cliffs overlooking wild ocean waves. Knights on horseback, armor glittering in the sunlight. Forests stretching out for miles. A giant of a man in a leather vest swinging a broad sword at her.

Julie gasped, broke the kiss and opened her eyes, half expecting to see that man. To feel the whistle of wind as the sword swept past her.

But there was only her and Kieran MacIntyre in the room. Everything—and nothing—was the same. God. Her body was still burning and her mind still filled with memories she knew didn't belong to her.

"What the *hell* was that?" she whispered, taking a step back from him.

He scrubbed one hand across his face, pulled in a long, deep breath and then blew it out again. His pale eyes met hers then shifted away. "Doesn't matter."

The nonanswer did nothing for her equilibrium.

When he looked back at her, his eyes were guarded, his features schooled into a stoic expression. "Get your things. We're leaving."

"I'm not going anywhere with you," she said, taking another step back.

"I can't protect you unless you're with me."

"Uh-huh. And what if it's *you* I need protecting from?"

"Damn it, you know that is not true."

"All I know is, you show up and my world goes to hell. Plus," she added, shaking her head, trying to dislodge the images still burned on her brain, "you're some kind of wacko hypnotist or something. Making me see things. Slipping into my mind…"

"I'm tele—"

"—pathic," she finished for him. "Yeah. So you said."

"This…connection between us is *not* my idea," he blurted, looking no more happy about the situation than she was.

"Fine. Great." She threw both hands high, then let them slap down to her sides again. "Whatever. I'm not interested in a connection of any kind with you." *Liar,* her brain whispered. "What I am interested in, is that you said earlier you knew who killed Alicia."

Just saying those words made her body sway as if she'd taken a punch to the stomach. Alicia. Dead. Dear God.

"You have to talk to the police."

"I can't."

"What do you mean you *can't?*" she demanded. "You have to!"

"It wouldn't do any good. They can't stop it."

"It?" This nightmare just got weirder by the minute.

"Never mind. It doesn't matter. Doesn't concern you."

"Of course it concerns me. My friend is *dead.* For all I know, Kate is, too."

"The police can't find it. Can't fight it. Only I can. Besides," he added dismissively, "they wouldn't believe me even if I told them the truth."

"If you won't tell them, I will," Julie said, disgusted with him. With herself. For God's sake, her friends had been attacked in their own home and she was kissing a man who at the very least was suspicious as hell.

He caught her as she stormed toward the door. "You can't."

"Watch me."

"This killer isn't something you're used to dealing with."

"Meaning what? Until you barged into my life I never had *any* dealings with a killer."

"The one who did this to your friends isn't human."

"I agree. He's an evil, vicious bastard."

"No." His mouth worked as if he were chewing on words trying to decide whether or not to say them. "That's not what I meant. I mean, it's not *human*."

"What?" Julie shook her head again. This just kept getting stranger and stranger. She took a half step toward her bedroom door, a vague plan taking shape in her mind. *Run to the police. They were still crawling over the living room. Help was only a few steps or one scream away. Don't stay here with a man who's obviously crazy.*

But on the other hand, she thought in the next moment, when he kissed her, she'd experienced memories and feelings that weren't even *hers*. So really, which one of them was the crazy one?

Kieran's pale blue eyes locked with hers, willing her to believe. To trust. His voice came low, soft, insistent. "This killer isn't a man at all. It's a demon."

"A demon."

"That's right."

"The Hell kind."

"Yes."

"Okay then," she said nodding. "Question answered. *You're* the crazy one."

Chapter 5

"I'm not crazy," Kieran told her, "but God help me, much more time with you and I may be."

"Very flattering, thanks," she said and walked a wide berth around him, headed toward the closet.

"I'm not trying to win your heart, woman," Kieran said, turning slowly to follow her movements. "I'm trying to keep you alive."

"Uh-huh." She grabbed a dark green suitcase, walked with it to the bed, then swung it up onto the mattress. Once it was there, she unzipped it, tipped the lid open and headed for a tall, mahogany chest of drawers. She pulled the first drawer wide, scooped in one hand and came out with a pile of panties and bras.

Kieran didn't even watch as she tossed them into the waiting suitcase. He didn't want to know that she wore pink or black or red underwear. He didn't need any more imagery for his already fevered brain to fixate on.

This hunt was not going as it was supposed to. As he stood here in the presence of a woman who threatened his equilibrium, the demon was most likely out selecting its next victim. He should be on its trail even now. And yet, he couldn't leave Julie Carpenter to fend for herself.

She had no idea just how dangerous this killer was. No clue that the world she existed in was only a portion of the story. If he told her about the different dimensions that lay alongside this one, each with its own versions of reality, she would think him more insane than she already did.

Not that he gave a damn what she thought of him. It was only that the more dangerous she thought he was, the less chance he would have of protecting her from the demon.

While these and a hundred other thoughts raced through his mind, Julie continued packing. She folded shirts and jeans and slacks, laying them neatly into the opened bag. Then she moved into the bathroom and he heard drawers being flung open and slammed shut. When she stepped out of the small room, she carried two bags, a hairdryer and several brushes.

"You should leave," she said, sparing him a quick, furtive glance.

"I'll leave when you do."

"What I do, where I go, is none of your business," she said, making an obvious effort to keep her voice steady and even.

"Woman, you try my patience."

"And stop calling me *woman*," she snapped, closing the suitcase and dragging the zipper around it with a sharp whiz of sound. "My name is Julie, you Neanderthal."

Kieran didn't want to use her name. It would give her too much importance. And he didn't want her to be important. If she *was* his Destined Mate, he wasn't interested. Since the night of his death at the hands of his wife's lover, Kieran had guarded his heart with the same staunch stoicism that he had guarded the portals between dimensions.

Never again would he allow a woman to so bewitch him that she could destroy him.

Never again would he allow his cock to do his thinking for him.

Swallowing back the instinctive need to keep her at bay, he said, "If you will not come to my home where I can keep you safe, I will at least see you to a hotel where the security is adequate."

She yanked the suitcase off her bed and staggered a little as it slapped into her legs. "You're not listening, sword man. I don't want your help. I don't need your help. I don't *trust* you."

That rankled. For centuries, he had stood guard over the mortal world. He'd earned the respect of his fellow Guardians. Had vanquished demons too numerous to count. Had delved into hells no man should have to think about in order to fulfill his duty.

And this woman didn't *trust* him?

Biting back the bitter words filling his mouth, he reached out, grabbed her suitcase and lifted it easily. "I don't need your trust. Just your obedience."

She snorted and folded her arms across her chest. Looking him up and down with a dismissive expression she said, "Look, just because you're a good kisser doesn't mean I'm looking to be your lapdog. Nobody tells me what to do, understand? I make my own decisions."

"Just as you decided on your own to lock your door last night?" he taunted her, moving close enough that she backpedaled a bit, trying for a safe distance. "Just as you decided to stay in this room?"

She flushed. "Fine. I listened to you last night—" she lifted one hand and jabbed her index finger at him. "But only because I was scared of *you*." Grabbing her suitcase from his grasp, she staggered again, set it down, and yanked up the pull handle. "And in case you haven't noticed, I'm not scared of you anymore."

"Yes, you are," he whispered and watched as her gaze jumped to meet his. "I can feel the waves of fear sliding from you now, as easily as I tasted your surrender when we kissed."

"Surrender?" She glanced around the room, shifting her gaze nervously, to anywhere but him. "Oh, please."

"You gave yourself to me in that moment," he said, moving in again and again until she was backed up against the wall and there was nowhere else for her to go. Kieran felt her fear and her desire, commingling into a near tangible aura that rippled from her and entangled him in its net. He strained against its allure even while tormenting her with its existence. Lifting one hand, he touched her cheek briefly, then let his hand drop away.

"You can deny it if you must, but we both know it's there. We both feel the draw of its strength."

She pulled in a long, shaky breath and steeled her expression before saying simply, "No."

His eyes narrowed. "A stubborn woman."

"You might want to keep that in mind."

Kieran nodded thoughtfully and kept his silence as she grabbed the handle on her suitcase.

"Now, I'm going to a hotel," she said, walking to the door without once giving him a backward glance. "Which I will choose on my own." She reached the door, put one hand on the doorknob and only then turned her head far enough to look at him. "I don't want to see you again."

"Yes," he said quietly, piercing her gaze with his own. "You do."

She swallowed hard. "Even if in some weird and twisted way, that's true…I'm not going to. I plan to stay as far away from you as possible."

Kieran bit back the urge to battle that statement. Continuing to argue with the woman would be futile. Whatever she thought of it, he would be watching her. Not only because of the danger hovering too nearby, but because if she *was* his Destined Mate, he might need her in this hunt.

By nightfall, Julie was locked into a hotel room, listening to the sound of her own heartbeat, wishing she weren't alone. Wishing she weren't so damn scared. Wishing...

"Stupid to wish at all," she muttered and moved to the windows, overlooking downtown L.A.

Usually when she wanted to get away from the house for a while, and get some work done in peace and quiet, she chose a closer hotel. One of the smaller, exclusive spots around Hollywood, like Château Marmont or the Sunset Towers. Tonight, though, was different. Tonight she was looking for big, anonymous, *safe*.

The Westin Bonaventure was a great hotel in anyone's estimation. Its five cylindrical glass towers made the hotel practically a landmark in a town that was known for splashy exhibitionism. But where a smaller boutique hotel specialized in the personal touch, the Bonaventure was too big for that. Here, she was just another guest. One of the thousands who zipped up and down in the glass elevators overlooking the city lights.

In the movie *True Lies*, Arnold Schwarzenegger and his "borrowed" police horse rode in those glass elevators to the roof in an attempt to catch a terrorist. But tonight, on the ride to her room, she hadn't been thinking about that movie scene. Instead she'd stared at the sea of lights spread out below her and wondered where the killer was.

And she was still wondering.

Demon.

Kieran had said that word so matter-of-factly that it still made Julie shake. Did he actually believe that? Was he as crazed as the killer that had splintered her world?

Wrapping her arms around herself, Julie scrubbed her hands over her upper arms, trying to ward off the chill that had been with her for hours.

It wasn't working.

"No one's watching me," she murmured, her gaze sweeping over the light-drenched darkness. But she couldn't shake the sensation of someone's gaze fixed on her. Taking a deep breath, she blew it out in a rush and tried to ease the knots still sliding through the pit of her stomach.

But the eerie sensation remained. The small hairs at the back of her neck lifted and she reached to smooth them down with her palm. Her heartbeat quickened into a gallop and she wondered if her life would ever again be the way it had been only yesterday?

"Perfect, Julie," she said, disgusted with herself. Alicia was dead, Kate was in ICU and *she* was feeling sorry for herself because she was scared.

Spinning away from the window, she snapped her drapes shut—a linen barrier against the dangers crouched beyond the glass. Then she walked to the phone, sat on the edge of the bed and quickly dialed a number she knew by heart.

The phone rang three times before a woman's voice said, "Hello?"

"Kenna?" Julie asked and heard the breathlessness in her own voice.

Kate's younger sister said, "Julie, honey, how you doin'?"

"Not so great," she admitted and twisted her index finger around the curly telephone cord. "Anything new on Kate?"

Kenna and her entire family were stationed in

the waiting room at the hospital. Julie would have been there, too, but she felt too... *guilty* for coming through the night unscathed while Kate lay quietly fighting for her life.

"No," Kenna admitted, her voice going to a whisper. "Hold on, I'm headed outside. The nurse is giving me the evil eye for using a cell phone in here."

A long minute passed before Kenna started talking again. "She's still unconscious, Julie. The docs are telling us that it's her body's way of healing itself. I don't know if I buy it, but they did upgrade her condition from critical to guarded."

"Good. That's good."

"Yeah, it is. But she looks terrible, Julie. Who knew us black women could look pale?"

"God, Kenna." Julie pulled her finger free of the cord, lifted her hand and shoved her hair back from her face.

"Sorry, sorry. I'm just...I don't know. Trying to make jokes to keep from screaming or kicking a wall or something. I just feel so damn helpless. You know?"

"Yeah," Julie said, knowing exactly how Kate's sister felt. "I do. Look, you should go back in to be with the family. But is it okay if I keep calling you to check on her?"

"Anytime, Jules. I'll keep you posted."

"Thanks." She sat on the bed, holding the damn phone long after Kenna hung up and the dial tone hummed in her ear.

Julie Carpenter was safe. For the moment. Kieran felt her doubts, her fears and closed his eyes as he stared up at the hotel tower. Focusing, he tried to calm her, to ease the terrors that would no doubt keep her up all night. But he couldn't reach her mind and after a moment or two, he gave it up.

Scowling, he realized that their connection wasn't strong enough yet for him to draw on the bond between them from a distance. Just as well, he thought. He didn't want the damn connection with her anyway.

At least she'd had the sense to leave her own neighborhood when she needed security. She was far enough away from the original kill site that hopefully the demon wouldn't bother tracking her. Yet Kieran couldn't count on that. With the free-ways linking every small corner of the city to its smaller boroughs, no spot was out of reach. She should have been ensconced in his home. At least then he would have been sure of her safety.

Hardheaded woman, he thought, eyes grim, mouth a tight slash of disapproval. She'd rather risk death than accept his help. But maybe that was for the best anyway. He surely didn't want her around. She only confused issues that should remain crystal clear.

Still, an annoying thought plagued him so that he couldn't quite turn his back on her completely. According to old Guardian legend, once he had sex with his Destined Mate, he would be able to telepathically link with the demon he was tracking—making it that much easier to capture.

Muttering a curse, he pushed one hand through his hair. This hunt was becoming more complicated all the time. For centuries, he'd stalked his prey, and he was always victorious. What's more, he'd done it without a Mate at his side.

Shifting his gaze from the glittering glass towers of the Bonaventure, he stared through the windshield and fired up the car's engine. Julie would be safe enough where she was. The demon hadn't followed her—that Kieran was sure of.

There was no scent lingering here. No smear of evil in the night air. Wherever the demon was now, it was concentrated on its next kill—not the sole survivor of its last one.

His phone rang in an obscenely chirpy tone and he yanked it out of his coat pocket and snapped it open. "Yes?"

"Ah, my friend," Santos said, his voice a low rumble of sound in the darkness, "you do not sound joyful. The demon still walks free?"

Frowning, Kieran shoved the car into gear, released the emergency brake and stepped on the gas. Steering the Lexus away from the Bonaventure, he moved into the swirl of traffic. "For the moment."

"That will change."

"Damned right it will."

"I have some information for you."

Kieran swung into a right turn, and headed down Figueroa. "What?"

"I called in a favor and got in touch with Rom."

Kieran blinked in surprise. Romulus Durant was one of the oldest of the Guardians. A Centurion in life, he had seen Millenia dawn and die—but he was notoriously private, avoiding other

Guardians, keeping to himself in a fortresslike palace outside Tuscany.

"How did you manage that?"

"It was not easy, my friend," Santos admitted with a sigh. "And now I owe a favor in return to Marguerite."

Kieran grinned, surprised that he could find a spark of humor in the disaster this day had become. "Not such a hardship, is it?"

"True," Santos admitted. "But she is a formidable warrior herself."

Marguerite LeClair, beautiful, deadly, had once been a spy—losing her life during World War I. Since then, she'd become one of the more fierce Guardians around.

Still, none of this was telling him what he wanted to hear. "What did Rom say about the Mate legends?"

"That they are all true. All of them."

Something in his chest tightened like a fist curling for a punch. He'd known it—almost from the instant of seeing Julie's picture months ago, Kieran had known that somehow their souls were entwined. The question was, would he allow that connection to grow?

Kieran frowned as he stopped for a red light and his grip on the phone tightened. All around him, neon signs made splashes of color in the darkness. His gaze locked on the pedestrians loping across the crosswalk and then shifted to take in the drivers on either side of him. Always watching. Always wary. The Guardian way.

How could a Guardian ever maintain the stoic watchfulness required if a Mate were alongside him? Foolish.

"Are you still there, my friend?"

"Yes."

"And are you willing now to tell me why the Mate legend is suddenly so important to you?"

"No." The light turned green and he stomped on the gas pedal, the car leaping ahead of the pack like a starving tiger moving in on a gazelle.

Santos laughed. "No matter. You have already told me much."

"Go kill something, Santos," Kieran muttered and hung up, stuffing his phone into his jacket pocket and taking a hard right again, heading up to the canyons overlooking the city.

Minutes flew by as he concentrated on the road and the coming task. He zipped in and out of traffic, ignoring the upraised fingers of irate drivers as he focused on the mission at hand. Time was short. The demon was still acclimating itself to this time, this world. And so, Kieran would have the advantage for a few days. He must make the most of it.

The night air rushed through the car and on that heavy wind, he caught a scent he'd been searching for. Hot and foul, it tasted sour, like bitter wine gone bad in the bottle. Kieran smiled to himself as he parked the car at the side of the road.

Here, in the canyons, the terrain was rough and the houses were fewer and farther between. Here darkness pooled in great, wide, empty patches and the night sky shone with stars that couldn't be seen under the city lights.

Kieran got out of the car, pocketing his keys, clutching his sword as he lifted his head to the wind and prepared to hunt.

He didn't need a Mate to do his job.

All he needed was the hate that kept him moving.

Chapter 6

Kieran stepped off the road and into the brush. From not far off came the sound of music sighing from a stereo. Moonlight sifted over his surroundings, coating everything in a faint, silvery glow.

Something scrabbled against the dirt but he didn't flinch. A small animal darting away from the scent of him didn't interest Kieran. He was after bigger game.

Scenting the air again, he closed his eyes, concentrated and searched for the demon's trail. When he picked it up, his eyes flashed open and narrowed as he crept up the hillside silent as a ghost. Cloaking himself as only a Guardian could, he moved unseen up the rocky hillside, stepping around brush and rocks, each stealthy step carrying him closer to his prey.

The trace energy left by the demon was thicker

here, as if it had lingered, pondering its next move. Kieran couldn't give it the time it wanted, needed for whatever its plans were. He had to end this soon. He didn't want to see another Whitechapel here, in Hollywood.

As he moved, the crickets quieted and the creatures who moved in darkness stilled—as if even the night itself were holding its breath, waiting for the violence to erupt again. The wind shifted and the trace elements he followed swirled around him in constantly changing patterns. But Kieran had had centuries to hone his tracking skills. He wouldn't be dissuaded now.

His boots ground into the rock-strewn dirt, his long legs carrying him up the hillside quickly. His breath was steady, his heartbeat slow, despite the adrenaline already coursing inside him. The hunt was all. The hunt had carried him through centuries.

This was what he knew.

This—pitting himself against a demon. He had been born and bred for battle. When alive, he'd served his Queen. As an Immortal, he served humanity—whether they knew it or not—and his own sense of duty.

Kieran's gaze narrowed, inspecting every shadow, every dip on the hillside. He paused, held his breath and listened with concentration for the slightest sound that might lead him to his quarry. But there was nothing.

Gritting his teeth, Kieran inhaled sharply, sensing that the trail was already going cold. He gripped his sword and let his gaze sweep the hills as he followed an increasingly fainter scent. The wisps of energy left by the demon were becoming slight, like an unraveling ribbon, losing their strength the higher he climbed.

All around him, houses on stilts jutted out from the hillsides. Patios bristled with lights and pools shone like puddles of turquoise. A door slammed, a car engine growled into life, a dog barked.

And Kieran fought a rising tide of bitterness as he neared the top of the hill. He wouldn't find the demon here, he knew that now. The damned thing was already gone, disappearing into the crowded night. But there was…something.

"Damn it." He let his sword arm drop as his gaze fixed on the body stretched out in the dirt before him.

A young man, Kieran guessed him to be no more than thirty, lay empty and dead atop the hill, wide eyes staring at a sky he could no longer see. A surprised expression was stamped forever on the man's features and Kieran couldn't help wondering why they always looked so stunned. Inviting a demon into your body was never going to end well—and yet, there were always those eager to experience it.

Going down into a crouch beside the body, Kieran squinted into the darkness and just caught a slight blurring of color outlining the corpse. A pitiful mockery of a rainbow, those hazy, indistinct colors always clung to a disposed-of body as the demon left it. And, since the remains of the demon's energy signature were still fading from the man's body, the demon hadn't been gone long.

Which meant, Kieran thought as he stood and let his gaze slide across the surrounding openness, he had missed the demon by only moments. The beast must have sensed his presence and decided to leave the body quickly.

And so it began.

Just as in Whitechapel.

Hopping from body to body, the demon would slash and torture its way through the city. It would bury itself in the heart and mind of any willing, dark soul and use it to commit the murders it craved. Even now, the demon was claiming someone new. Somewhere in the city, a human was welcoming the demon into their body, feeding on the demon's strength and rage as surely as it fed from them.

Kieran slid his sword back into the scabbard at his side with a whisper of steel on steel. There was nothing more to be learned here. The body was no more than an empty vessel now, its original owner already on his way to hell.

The demon could be anywhere and Kieran would now have to wait to track it. To wait for the next murder. The next clue. The next hint of trace energy staining the air.

He glanced down at the dead man who had hosted the demon while it killed and shook his head. "You were a fool. And now you're paying. If you know what's good for you," he added as he turned to stride back down the hill to where his car waited, "you'll go back to hell where you belong."

Julie disconnected from the Internet and closed her laptop. Two days she'd been at the Bonaventure and it already felt like two years. The room was too small to even enjoy pacing. She felt as though she were in a cage and yet she couldn't make herself leave, either.

Is this what it would be like from now on? Would she always live in fear? She didn't like it. Didn't like feeling powerless and on edge. Didn't want to become the kind of person who hid from life because of the terrors that *might* happen.

And yet, she'd already lived through a close call that very few people ever experienced. A killer had walked through her home. Had killed one friend and grievously injured the other. *Could* have killed Julie.

"Why didn't he?" she asked aloud of the empty room. Picking up a pencil, she tapped the eraser end against a stack of papers. The steady thumping sound was almost like another heartbeat and she was desperate enough to almost pretend it was. Better than being alone.

Shaking her head, she tossed the pencil down and tried to understand how she had escaped injury that night. Was it only because of Kieran's warnings? Had hiding in her room behind a locked door really kept her safe? Or was Alicia the target all along and she would have been safe no matter what?

There were weird people in the world, she knew that. As a reporter, she'd done plenty of stories on them. And Alicia *had* been an actress. She'd been in a dozen or more TV shows—small parts, but wasn't that enough for a crazed stalker to fixate on her? Had Kate just been an afterthought? Wrong place, wrong time?

"Oh God." This wasn't helping. She wasn't accomplishing anything and that made her nuts. She was far more used to doing something. To working. To digging into a situation and figuring it out from all angles.

She laid one hand on the stack of paper on the desk. Her portable printer had been pretty damn busy over the last couple of days. She'd punched Kieran MacIntyre's name into the Internet and had followed every thread she'd been given. There were always pockets of information to be mined. Always secrets to be revealed and truths to be uncovered.

Yet she'd found surprisingly little on the reclusive gazillionaire. Nothing on a family. Where he grew up. How he'd amassed his fortune.

"But on the upside," she muttered as she stood and walked to the wide windows, "no mention of him being a psycho, either." She'd gone as deep in her search as she was able and had found no mention of psychiatric troubles, brushes with the law…*nothing*.

Which was just a little infuriating to the reporter inside her. There was always information. Always. People didn't live a life and leave no mark. And yet, Kieran MacIntyre appeared to have managed just that.

She pulled back the edge of the draperies she kept closed and hungrily stared at the world outside, like a prisoner being led out of solitary confinement for an hour in the yard. Sunset stained the sky with deep colors of gold and rose, painting the edges of the high, dark clouds that had threatened—but not delivered—rain all day.

Somewhere out there, the killer was going about his life. Maybe sitting in a restaurant. Or going to a movie. Or was locked in a traffic jam on the 405. He would be thinking about the murders. Enjoying the memories.

Julie shivered and her fingers curled tightly into the sand-colored, heavy polyester drapes. He was free, moving around the city, and *she* was trapped in a hotel room, terrified.

Yeah, that was fair.

"Nothing about this is fair," she reminded herself. "Kate doesn't deserve to be in the hospital and Alicia doesn't deserve to be *dead*."

The hotel TV was tuned to the news and she turned to watch when she heard the newscaster mention the words "Hollywood Slasher."

Alicia's picture flashed on the screen following a shot of the first woman who'd been found dead on Hollywood Boulevard. Julie wrapped her arms around her middle, held her breath and listened as the indifferent anchor read the information and even managed to *smile* at his audience.

"A few dead women mean nothing more than a story to them," Julie said, disgusted both with the news guy for his cavalier attitude and herself for watching. She picked up the remote, flicked the TV off and winced at the sudden silence of the room. She was never going to make it here. She couldn't stay in this hotel room, wondering what the hell was going on out there. She had to *do* something. Anything.

Maybe she should have told the police about MacIntyre. About his warning. About his damn *sword,* for God's sake. But she hadn't. Something instinctive had kept her silent and now, she wondered if she'd done the right thing.

A knock on her door startled her enough that she jumped, then laughed at herself for the nerves pulsing inside. "Probably just the room service guy," she muttered, walking to the door and pausing before opening it to peer through the peephole.

Pale blue eyes looked back at her, their intensity rocking her back on her heels even as a wild rush of something she didn't want to explore too fully filled her.

"Open the door."

Kieran's deep voice rumbled through the door and seemed to dance on every one of her nerve endings. Julie's fingers shook and her heartbeat quickened into a hard, slamming gallop in her chest.

"What do you want?" Stall, she thought, even while she was reaching to undo the locks.

"Woman, I need to talk to you and I don't intend to do it from the hall. Open the door or I will."

She swallowed hard, her hand stilling on the flip lock at the top of the door. *What kind of moron*

would it make her if she let this man into her
room? A killer was loose out there and for all she
knew it was him.

But even as that thought jolted through her
brain, she argued the point. He wasn't the killer.
He'd had plenty of time and opportunity to kill her
the night of the party—not to mention the following day.

Maybe, though, her brain warned, this is the
plan. Maybe he likes getting women to trust him
before he kills them.

"Then I'm safe," she murmured. "Because I
don't trust him."

Still watching him through the peephole, she
saw his eyes narrow and a muscle in his jaw twitch
with an angry jump. She could practically *see* him
vibrating with banked strength, power and frustration. After a long moment, he sighed and said
tightly, "Yes. You *do* trust me. You don't want to.
But you do."

That pushed her into action. Jumping away
from the door, she angrily slammed the lock off,
opened the door and glared at him. "Stay out of
my mind, okay?"

He walked past her, stepping into the room and

making it seem to shrink in size by his very presence. She slammed the door behind him, wincing at the blast of sound. He stood in the center of the room, gaze sliding around the impersonal space as if searching for a danger she hadn't noticed yet.

"I did not have to listen to your thoughts to know you trust me," he said, turning slowly to face her. "You haven't told the police about me."

"Maybe I was waiting for the right time."

"You're not. You won't tell them anything."

"You seem pretty sure of yourself," she snapped, leaning back against the door and folding her arms across her chest in what she knew was a classic defensive pose.

His eyes were implacable. Pale and cold, they were filled with shadows of thoughts she couldn't read. Didn't want to understand. And yet she felt better having him here. Oh God, she'd been alone too long. Alone, her thoughts had room to roam and an unlimited imagination to feed on.

Danger clung to him like a lover—but she didn't feel personally threatened. Was she fooling herself? Was she making a deadly mistake just allowing him to get this close to her?

"What do you want?" she asked, unfolding her arms and shoving her hands into the pockets of her jeans. "Why are you here?"

"To get you out of here."

Only a few minutes ago, she'd been longing for the same damn thing. Now, though, she instantly went on the offensive. "I'm not going anywhere."

"I cannot keep hunting the demon while protecting you here."

"You've been—" Her mouth dropped open.

"Watching you, yes."

She'd felt unseen eyes on her every time she peered through the drapes, which is exactly why she'd been keeping them closed. But hearing him admit that he'd been watching was a little unsettling.

"Why?"

"You know why," he said shortly. "The killer is aware of you. You're in danger."

A cold hand closed around her heart and a bone-deep chill swept through her. "From the killer, not from you."

"That's right."

"How do I know that?"

"I will not play this unamusing game with

you again, Julie Carpenter." He moved so quickly she hardly caught the blur of action. And then he was standing in front of her, his hands on her upper arms, his fingers digging into her skin beneath her charcoal-gray cashmere sweater.

Pulling her up and away from the door, his grip on her tightened and his gaze speared into hers. "You know I am no threat to you. I can protect you. But not while you're here."

On her toes, she struggled for balance, but knew she wouldn't find it. Even if she was flat-footed and steady on the floor, having his hands on her, his gaze locked with hers, she wouldn't feel steady. The scent of him, a spicy cologne, leather and *male* filled her, clouding her mind, fogging her judgment.

Heat flashed from his hands into her arms to ricochet around inside her chest like a fireball. Her breath strangled in her chest, her throat tightened and her mouth went dry. She stared into his eyes and swore she could see a soul as old as time.

What?

"Only I can protect you," he said, his breath warm on her face.

"Why should I believe that?" she heard herself say and silently congratulated herself on being able to speak at all.

"Because you know I told you the truth before. This killer is a demon. Only I can find it. Only I can keep you safe from it."

"I don't believe in demons," she said quietly. "Evil, yes. But not demons."

"They are as real as you and I," he said and pulled her even closer, his mouth now only a breath from hers. "And this one will not be stopped until I stop it."

His eyes caught her and like a master hypnotist, he eased her with a look. Calmed her with a touch. Heated her with his voice.

Julie lifted both hands, laying them palms flat on his chest. The cool of his black leather coat beneath her hands felt real. Solid. The beating of his heart assured her he was human, despite what he insisted his quarry was.

In the last few days, her entire world, everything she knew and counted on had been changed irrevocably. And in the ashes that were her life now, Kieran MacIntyre was the only thing that made sense anymore.

How twisted was that?

"Will you come with me?"

She couldn't stay in the hotel indefinitely. She couldn't go home.

There was really only one choice left.

"Yes."

Having her this close to him was a distraction Kieran couldn't afford. But he had little choice in the matter. The demon had switched bodies and it had been two days since its last kill, so there was no trail to follow. He would have to wait until the beast made its next move before finding its scent again.

For now, all he could do was settle Julie where he knew she would be safe and continue to stalk the hills and alleys surrounding Hollywood.

"How long have you lived here?" she asked as a pair of high, scrolled iron gates swung open at the approach of his car.

"A long time." He wouldn't give her more. She wouldn't believe him if he told her the truth and besides, he had no interest in giving her even more information. Destined Mate or not, he had no place for her in his life. If he could use her to make his powers stronger, to help him track and capture the demon, all well and good.

But the thought of an eternity with a Mate left him cold.

He steered the car along the narrow, tree-lined driveway as it climbed the hill overlooking Los Angeles. Fifty years he'd lived in this house, long enough that now, to keep rumors from spreading and growing, he was pretending to be his own son. Immortality was fine in its way. But stay in one place too long and there were questions asked that had no answers.

Another gate yawned open at the top of the hill and swung closed behind him as he drove through, approaching the house.

"Not much for visitors, are you?" she asked.

He glanced at her in the dim light and saw a wry smile curving her mouth.

"No."

"Well, that was honest, anyway."

"Here is more honesty for you," he said as he steered around the last curve of the driveway and parked before a massive home that looked more like an ancient Scottish fortress than a home in Hollywood. "If you attempt to write any type of story about me, my home or anything else you see while you're here—I'll sue. You and your newspaper."

Both of her dark red eyebrows lifted. "Gee. Honest *and* friendly. Look, I'm not here as a reporter, so chill out, okay?"

"Fine." He shut off the engine and opened his door. Pausing, he said, "Go inside. I will bring your bags."

She stepped out of the car and whistled, low and long as she swept her gaze over the home that he'd had built so many years before. Kieran moved to the trunk, reached in and got her bag, then closed it again.

He watched her as she studied his home and he tried to see it as she was, with fresh eyes. Hewn gray stone climbed for three stories. Leaded glass windows sparkled with lamplight. Tower rooms on all four corners of the building boasted wide, unobstructed views of the valley and the city sprawling at the foot of the hill. And on the roof, actual battlements jutted up from the stone, giving him a place to walk, to think, to be under the stars while planning his next hunt.

She swiveled her head to look at him. "This is amazing."

He gave her an abrupt nod. "Thank you."

She followed him as he headed up the flag-stone steps toward the wide, oak double doors. "I can't believe I've never seen a picture of this place. Architectural magazines alone would love to photograph it."

He glanced at her over his shoulder. "This is my home. It is not a curiosity."

"You're wrong," she said, taking the steps while craning her head back to admire the sweep of stone and glass. "It's both. If people knew what this place was like…"

He stopped dead and she ran right into him. His gaze fixed on hers, he waited, silent.

Finally she held up both hands. "Fine. Right. No stories. No pictures."

Nodding, he flung the door open and stepped back for her to precede him inside. She did and a sigh of appreciation sifted to him on the lemon oil scented air.

Electric light spilled from the library on the left, into the marble-floored entry. Framed paint-ings almost as tall as Kieran lined the walls that hugged each side of a hallway that appeared at least a mile long. An elegant swirl of crystal held an immense bouquet of sterling roses on a small polished table at the foot of the enormous stone staircase leading upstairs.

Julie spun in a slow circle, taking it all in, her mouth hanging wide, her eyes sparkling with delight as she noted every detail. And surprisingly, Kieran felt a sharp stab of pleasure seeing her appreciation of the home he loved.

"This is…*awesome*," she said, her gaze finally shifting to him. Her smile was bright, her eyes wide as she said, "Really. It's just amazing."

"Thank you." He carried her bags up the stairs and she followed just a step or two behind him, her tennis shoes silent on the stone.

On the second floor, he walked to the fourth door on the right, then swung it open and stepped back. Julie walked inside and stopped just over the threshold.

At first glance of the house, she'd been stunned into near speechlessness. Now, that feeling only multiplied. The walls were painted a soft, dreamy blue and a cherrywood, four-poster bed wide enough for five people to sleep in comfortably was the focal point.

More roses were here, sitting atop a dressing

table with a mirror reflecting their beauty right behind them. A private bath snaked off one side of the room and as she moved to take a look, she wasn't surprised to see the luxuriously appointed bathroom was twice the size of her entire bedroom suite at home. Green and white tiles covered the floor and the shower enclosure. A sage-green whirlpool tub sat beneath a bank of windows and a long sweep of counter held a wicker basket filled with shampoos and guest soaps that put five-star hotels to shame.

Turning around, she watched Kieran drop her bags onto the big bed and then spare her a quick look. "You should be comfortable here."

"Yeah," she said, glancing around the room and noting with pleasure the private terrace nearly hidden behind sheer curtains. "I think so."

Nodding again, he said only, "Settle in. Dinner is in an hour."

Then he left her alone and as she walked to the French doors and opened them, walking out onto the stone terrace, she wondered if it would be possible to "settle in." After all, she hardly knew him. Sure, she hadn't found anything awful about him on the Internet, but how much did that mean, really?

A breath of cold air slipped past her and a chill snaked along her spine, making her shiver.

At the hotel, she'd felt as though she were in a cage. Here…she turned around, rested one hip on the stone balustrade and looked in at her gloriously appointed bedroom. Wasn't this a cage, too? An even more difficult one to escape?

Had she done the right thing, trusting Kieran MacIntyre to keep her safe?

Or had she jumped from the frying pan into an inferno?

Chapter 7

The beast moved restlessly through the movie theater. Changing seats three times before finally settling behind a pretty young redhead who smelled of flowers and...promise. Around him, people muttered then settled down to watch the film flickering into life on the screen.

Interesting, yes. But the beast had other, more important things to think about than bits of film. The Guardian had been close tonight. Close enough that the beast had been forced to flee its host's body much earlier than it had planned. Though truly, it mused, running one hand over its new host's chest, the change had been for the better. This body was taller, stronger and more comely. All for the best, it told itself.

MacIntyre was good, but after a century and more of planning, the beast was better.

And it would not be denied its pleasures.

In the seat ahead of the beast, the woman threw her head back and laughed at something on the screen. The beast's gaze locked on the curve of her neck and it, too, began to laugh.

Julie stepped into the biggest kitchen she'd ever seen. Gleaming stainless steel appliances crowded the walls and at least an acre of black granite countertops shone under the fluorescent lights. The walls were a dark brick red, almost matching the bricks in the massive hearth on the far wall.

Even California got a little chilly in January, and just looking at the flames snapping and licking at the tree-size logs made Julie feel warmer.

A fireplace.

In the kitchen.

Oh, yeah, she thought. She could get used to a place like this. Even if it was huge. She'd gotten lost twice on her way to dinner. Not surprising in a place as big as a castle.

"This is amazing," she said, glancing at Kieran as he closed a restaurant-size refrigerator with a bump from his hip.

"Thank you." He set down an enormous blue

glass bowl filled with potato salad and another, the same size, of pasta salad.

Already sitting in the middle of an antique walnut table, was a platter piled high with golden fried chicken—the scent of which had led her to the kitchen. Still, "This isn't what I was expecting."

One black eyebrow lifted. "You don't like chicken?"

"No," she said, moving to stand closer to the fire. "That's not it. It's just—" she lifted both hands and waved them, indicating the entire house "—a place like this. So old-worldly, so—I don't know. Fried chicken and potato salad just seem a little ordinary."

"Don't knock it," a deep voice came out of nowhere and Julie jumped, startled, as a tall, broad man wearing blue jeans and a dark T-shirt that read Navy SEAL came in from outside.

"Nathan Hawke," Kieran said, "Julie Carpenter. She'll be staying here for a while."

"Pleasure," the big man said, though from the grim set of his features, she didn't think he meant it. "As for the food, it looks great. First decent meal I've had since I got here."

"Meaning?" she asked.

He shook his head as he walked to the sink,

turned on the water and washed his hands. "Usually we're sitting in a dining room for fifty and it's salmon flown in from the Highlands. Or lobster flown in from Maine. Goose liver and snails, for God's sake. About time we got some real food."

Kieran stiffened, glared at the other man then shifted a look at Julie. "I thought you would be more comfortable in here."

Sure, she thought. The peasant would be more comfy in a kitchen with picnic food. Don't make her squirm by expecting her to have table manners. For God's sake. The man was from another century.

Kieran reached into the fridge for a bottle of wine. As he opened it, he nodded at the table. "Ignore him," he said. "Sit. Eat."

"Wow. So gracious." She took a chair closest to the fireplace, still fighting a bone-deep chill. She sat down and reached for a piece of chicken. "I'm guessing you didn't cook this."

A harsh, short laugh shot from Nathan's throat as he took a seat opposite her.

"My housekeeper does the cooking," Kieran said, doing a good job of ignoring the other man himself.

Nathan began heaping food onto his plate in a way that told Julie there wouldn't be many left-overs. She looked from one man to the other and wondered what the hell was going on? The two men couldn't be more different from each other. Was Nathan a roommate? Family? Boarder?

She almost laughed aloud at that thought. A man who lived in a freaking castle wouldn't need to rent out rooms.

Kieran took a seat beside her and she somehow managed to stop a shiver of something delicious from making her sigh.

"So," she said into a silence that was beginning to wear on her, "are you guys old 'friends'?"

Nathan glanced at Kieran and shrugged. "I've been here awhile now."

"Uh-huh. And is there something I should know about..." Her voice trailed off. An uncomfortable question and judging by the way Kieran kissed, she was willing to bet he was as straight as a ruler. Still, two gorgeous men, living in a castle, cut off from everyone else...well, this was Hollywood after all and better to know right up-front.

Kieran frowned at her. "What do you mean?"

Nathan choked on a piece of chicken. Shaking

his head, he said, "No way, lady. I live here. That's all."

"Good to know." Not that it mattered, she thought, taking a spoonful of potato salad before the two men devoured it all. She wasn't here to be romanced, for pity's sake. She was here because a psycho killer might be after her.

The fire at her back sent warmth scuttling through her system and when Kieran's arm brushed her bare forearm, her skin prickled as if from an electrical charge. She shouldn't have changed out of her sweater into a short-sleeved silk blouse. Just for her own peace of mind, she eased away from him.

He noticed and frowned.

Too bad.

"So, what do you guys do?" she asked, breaking another silence. "I mean for a living."

"No questions," Kieran said firmly, giving her a look designed to quell the fainthearted. Then he shot another look at Nathan. "She's a reporter."

"Ah…" The other man nodded and looked at her as if she belonged on a glass slide under a microscope. A moment later, he dismissed her and turned to Kieran. "Santos called while you were out. Seemed to think it was important."

"I'll call him."

"Who's Santos?" Julie tried, not really expecting an answer.

"A friend," Kieran said and leaned across her to get the bottle of wine.

He did it on purpose, she knew. That long reach, his forearm brushing against her breasts and lighting up her insides like a fireworks show at Disneyland. Her nipples were tingling and her blood was humming.

For God's sake, it was only a *touch*.

"Look," she said, a little more abruptly than she might have if she hadn't been on a slow simmer, "I agreed to come here, but I'm not going to be treated like a prisoner."

"No one has treated you as a prisoner," Kieran argued.

"I'm not allowed to ask questions," she reminded him.

"On the contrary, you may ask all the questions you wish. You simply will not receive answers."

Nathan snorted and she fired a glare at him.

Firelight played on Kieran's features, shifting shadow and light across his face and into his eyes.

It was hypnotic, she thought and forced herself to look away from him.

You are safe here.

Julie jumped and her gaze snapped back to his. "I told you to quit doing that," she said tightly. "I don't want you in my mind."

He shrugged. "Then prevent it."

"How?"

A smile curved his mouth and she almost fell off her chair in surprise. The man should really smile more often. Of course, if he did, she might be in even bigger trouble.

"No questions answered," he said, clearly enjoying her fluster.

This was great. She'd been an idiot for coming here with him.

"You know what?" she said, pushing up and away from the table suddenly, "I'm done. Thanks for dinner." She turned for the back door, then stopped. "Oh. Is it all right with *you* if I go outside?"

He nodded briefly. "Stay on the grounds."

"And just how would I get past your iron welcome gate anyway?" she muttered and yanked the door open. She slammed it shut behind her and silence dropped onto the kitchen for several long minutes.

Finally Nathan looked at his friend. "Why'd you bring her here? I know I'm new to the whole Guardian thing. But I thought we were supposed to keep a low profile. Secrecy and all that shit."

Kieran blew out a breath, picked up his glass and drained what was left of his chilled white wine. Setting the glass down again, he looked at the man across from him.

Nathan Hawke had been dead only three years. He was very new to the Guardians, and according to tradition was being trained by a more experienced Guardian. In this case, Kieran.

As a Navy SEAL, Nathan already possessed the skills that would see him through eternity. Now all he really needed to learn was how to use that training to hunt demons.

"She's a reporter for God's sake," Nathan said, waving one hand at the closed door and the backyard beyond. "Isn't that asking for trouble?"

"Yes and no," Kieran sighed, suddenly feeling every one of his four hundred and sixty-four years. "Because of *what* she is, she'll ask questions and try to dig for truths. Because of *who* she is, she won't use whatever she finds."

"You're sure about that?" Nathan looked less than convinced.

"I'm sure," he said, pushing up from the table and heading for the back door. "Clear this up when you're finished. Mrs. Rosen won't let either one of us live if the kitchen's a mess when she wakes up."

"We're immortal," Nathan reminded him with a rare smile.

"And she can make eternity a nightmare if she chooses. Clean it up." Without another word, Kieran opened the back door and stepped out onto the flagstone patio.

Full grown trees ringed the yard and house, towering over the battlements, shielding the property from curious eyes. There were other impressive homes in the area he knew, and most of them were at least partially visible from the freeways or from the hilltops. But when Kieran had built this place, he'd planned ahead.

Pines, oaks, maples, the tallest trees he could find were all planted strategically, ensuring him of the solitude he knew was necessary if he were to keep his identity a secret. Yes, he was known as a philanthropist. He had no trouble donating money to worthy causes. Besides helping others, it gave him enough of a cloak of mystery that most people respected his privacy. Mainly because they didn't want to risk pissing him off and ending his donations.

It all had worked well for more than fifty years.

Until Julie Carpenter entered his life.

His gaze, as sharp in the darkness as in daylight, swept the yard, noting every shrub, every flower, every fountain and bench. All was as it should be.

Then he spotted her, at the edge of the lawn, sitting on a redwood bench below an oak tree he'd imported half grown from Scotland. A memory of his life. A reminder of how that life had ended.

As if he needed one.

He set off across the patio and stepped onto neatly manicured grass. His housekeeper and her husband, the gardener, had been with him for forty years. They were aware of the Guardians, having both been born into families who took oaths of loyalty and service to the cause. When the Rosens became too old or infirm to work, they would retire to a home Kieran had ready for them in the Bahamas. And their son and his wife would move into the castle and continue to help the Guardians.

His footsteps were faint on the damp grass. He could have obfuscated himself, slipped up on her unaware. But he didn't think she could take many more jolts of surprise. As much as it irritated him, the turns his life had taken in the last few days, he reminded himself that *her* life was in even more turmoil.

She was unprepared for the kind of things she was now facing. And though it shamed him to admit it, he hadn't made it any easier for her.

She looked up when he approached and lurched to her feet as though she was about to sprint away. Then she changed her mind, lifted her chin and said shortly, "Even a prisoner is entitled to a little privacy."

"You're not a prisoner."

"No? Don't leave the grounds? Isn't that what you said a few minutes ago?"

"It's for your own safety."

"And just how do I know I'm safe *here?*"

"You feel it."

"Don't tell me what I feel."

"I shouldn't have to," he said, walking closer, one small step at a time, as if trying to sneak up on a wild animal ready to bolt.

"Why won't you answer my questions?"

"You know why. You're a reporter."

"I gave you my word I wouldn't write about any of this," she said, insult humming around her. "Besides, who would I write it for? A ghost magazine? *Psychotic Monthly*? Nobody would ever believe any of this." She stopped, ran one hand through her hair and muttered, "Even I don't believe it and I'm living it."

Kieran heard the whisper of confusion in her voice. The very real edge of not despair, but *surrender,* and it bothered him. Scowling, he realized that he had admired her formidable nature even as it had annoyed him. And now, seeing that strong foundation shake even a little, was troubling.

He held out one hand. "Come with me."

She looked from his hand to his eyes and asked, "Why?"

"Woman, must you have a question for everything? Is there no risk-taking in your blood?"

"Well pardon the hell out of me," she snapped.

"It's been a rough couple of days in case you've forgotten."

Nearly growling in frustration, he simply asked, "Will you come?"

She hugged her arms around her middle against the chill of the January night and considered him for a long minute. While she was thinking, Kieran slipped off his long-sleeved black shirt, stepped close and laid it over her shoulders.

"What's that for?"

"You're cold," he said, holding out his hand again.

She shimmied into the shirt, sliding her arms into sleeves that hung well over the backs of her hands. The warmth from his body, his scent, clung to the fabric, making her warmer than she would have been wrapped up in a cashmere blanket. Then she looked at him, bare chested in the moonlight and asked, "You're not cold?"

A slight smile curved his mouth and disappeared again in an instant. "No." She kept watching him, curiosity shining in her eyes, so he granted her a small boon and added, "I'm Scottish. A California 'winter' is no colder than one of our soft, summer days."

Julie laid her hand in his and when his fingers closed around hers, she said, "Thanks."

"For…?"

"Actually answering a question with more than a single word."

He smiled again and instantly frowned when he realized it. Kieran couldn't remember smiling as much in the last twenty years as he had in the last hour. She was changing things, whether she meant to or not and he wasn't happy with that knowledge.

"How do you do that?" she asked as he started walking back toward the house, leading her through the darkness with unerring steps.

"Do what?"

"Go from a smile to a scowl in less than a heartbeat?"

"More questions?"

"No more answers?"

He opened the back door, nodded to Nathan, still at the table, and turned left and kept walking, taking her up the staircase behind a pantry stocked with enough food to feed them all for months.

"Wow," she murmured as she started up the wide, stone steps, "you're ready for a siege, aren't you?"

"Again, questions."

"Again," she retorted, a laugh in her voice, "no answers."

"You are an infuriating woman, Julie Carpenter."

"That's been said before," she admitted, keeping pace with his long legs as they climbed and climbed and climbed. "Where are we going?"

His grip on her hand tightened. "Patience."

"Hello. Maybe you haven't met me. I'm Julie and I don't do patience."

"Yes, I have noticed," he said, stopping on a landing at the top of the house.

Julie glanced down the long hall behind them. Wall sconces shaped like old-fashioned gaslights spilled a warm, golden glow on the polished wood floor. Paintings lined these walls too and when she spotted a Monet, she wondered if it was an original.

Considering the man's seemingly staggering wealth, she was willing to bet it was. Amazing. The sumptuous decor. The castle.

The man.

He opened a heavy wood door, arched at the top, and stepped back to allow her to precede him. Yet another flight of stairs awaited her, but these led to the roof. Overhead, the stars swam brightly in a sky so wide, so black, it seemed endless. Julie lifted her face into a cold wind that slapped at her as she climbed to the stone roof and turned in a slow circle, admiring the sweeping views surrounding her.

"Oh, my God…"

Over the tops of the trees, she could see an ocean of lights, stretching out for miles. There were so many lights, the horizon seemed to blur with the glow of them. The wind brushed through the trees, making the pine needles whisper and the bare branches of the oaks and maples clatter, sounding like old women laughing.

Julie walked slowly across the rooftop and for a moment, felt as though she'd stepped back in time. She could almost hear the clank of armor, the whistle of arrows slicing through the air. She was half convinced if she leaned over the battlements, she would see knights training in the yard below.

Turning, she watched Kieran walk toward her and a quick flash of something hot and wild and completely overwhelming surged through her. Moonlight gleamed on his bare chest, highlighted his long, black hair and glinted in his dark eyes. The man moved with a stealthy sort of grace that made her think of panthers or stalking tigers.

And now she knew exactly how a gazelle might feel in this same situation.

Who *was* he?

There was so much more here than she knew. So much more to him than she could even guess. She hadn't forgotten that he'd said the killer he was searching for was a *demon*. So what did that make him? Crazy? And what did it make *her* for being here alone with him?

When he was close enough, he looked into her eyes. "You're wondering about me."

Julie stiffened. "I told you to stay out of my mind."

"There's no need to read your thoughts when your expression says clearly what you are thinking."

"Swell. So much for my reporter's 'poker face.'"

"There is a connection between us," he said, his voice a low rumble of sound that seemed to echo in the stillness. "Whether either of us is happy about that or not. You cannot hide your feelings from me."

"I can try," she said, despite knowing that he was probably right.

"And will, I've no doubt. But for now, come. I want to show you something."

Her eyebrows lifted high on her forehead. "There's *more?*"

Another brief smile and Julie felt her knees melt. Seriously, the man was too powerful for his own good. Or hers, for that matter.

"Yes, there's more." He took her hand and led her to the far edge of the roof where a very state-of-the-art looking telescope sat beneath a clear, protective tarp.

"This seems so out of place here," she murmured as he pulled off the tarp and spent a few minutes aligning the telescope with the heavens. "So…modern."

He flicked her a quick look and gave her that all too brief smile again. "There's no reason to not appreciate both the past and the future."

"Wow," Julie said, leaning against the cold stone battlement behind her. "A Renaissance man."

His eyes flashed. "More than you know."

"What else don't I know about you?" she mused more to herself than to him, since she knew darn well he wouldn't be answering.

"Too much," he said softly, then shook his head as if brushing away her questions. "Now come and take a look."

She walked closer and let him guide her to the telescope, his hands at her waist feeling warm and strong and compelling. Bending slightly, she looked into the eyepiece and her breath left her in a rush. "Oh, it's so beautiful."

"It is."

Through the telescope, the moon looked close enough to touch. It glowed with an un-earthly light and seemed to shimmer in the blackness. The last couple of days, the fears, the worries, the unsettled feeling of not knowing what to do next inexorably drained away, leaving her with nothing more than a sense of awe. For the universe.

For life.

Slowly, reluctantly, Julie tore herself from the image and straightened up to look at him. She stared at him thoughtfully for a long moment before saying, "You're an interesting man, Kieran Mac-Intyre. Recluse. Gazillionaire. Sword-carrying tracker of 'demons.' Amateur astronomer. Anything else?"

"A few things," he admitted, moving in close to her. Close enough that she caught his scent, heavy on the cool breeze drifting past her. It seemed to wrap itself around her, threatening to drown her in sensation.

"Anything you'd care to share?" she whispered, wincing a little when her soft voice broke under the strain of having her throat close up.

"Perhaps," he allowed and bent his head to hers.

This wouldn't solve anything, she told herself even as she went up on her toes and leaned into him.

And at the moment, she couldn't have cared less.

Chapter 8

The moment his mouth took hers, Kieran felt the threads already binding them, tighten. Even though he had thought himself prepared to experience the connection with a would-be Destined Mate again, he felt the world shift beneath his feet.

Simply touching her, tasting her, filled him with emotions and sensations he hadn't known in too many years to consider. Nearly overcome, he groaned, feeding on the rush of desire that clawed and clutched at his insides. He wanted her desperately, with a sudden, fierce longing that almost knocked him off his feet.

A small, insistent voice at the back of his mind warned him to stop. To take a mental step back. To hold her at a distance and keep their connection at a minimum. To use her strictly for the renewed strength and power she could afford him. But he wasn't listening to that sage, logical voice.

Instead he opened himself completely to the connection flashing through him, allowing her thoughts to burst into his mind, staggering him with their jagged, splintered, illogical pattern. Her mind was as wild and untamed as the woman herself. She was filled with color—*life.*

His tongue tangled with hers. Her hands fisted in his hair, tugging, pulling him closer, more tightly to her. His arms came around her middle and held her length pressed to his. He felt every curve, every line of her body as if it were on fire, burning itself into him until he wasn't sure where she left off and he began.

And their connection deepened.

Kieran hissed in a breath, as the onslaught of all Julie was battered its way into his solitary existence, and still he couldn't break the kiss. He had to have more of her. She moaned into his mouth and that soft sigh of sound whispered through him with a flash of need and hunger like nothing he'd ever known before.

He tipped her head back, cradling it in his palm, as he devoured her, taking all she had to offer—

silently demanding that she give him even more. He was like a starving man suddenly served a banquet fit for a king.

And the rush of color, thought, memory, solidified in his mind.

Desire. Fear. Uncertainty.

And images of another man.

Jealousy tore through him like shards of glass, slicing at his soul—until he realized what her memories were showing him.

Betrayal.

The man she'd once loved leaving her for another woman.

A friend.

He tasted Julie's tears.

Choked on her fury and shared it.

Pride raced in next, at her joy in rebuilding her life. Making a success of a career she loved.

And then fear roared through her more powerfully than before. Fear of him. Fear of what lay crouched in the shadows.

Fear of what she felt.

Their bond chained them in a tight knot of passion, neither of them able or willing to break free. He shifted her in his arms, sliding one hand up beneath the hem of her shirt, needing to feel the smooth sweep of her skin against his.

A cold, sharp wind swept over the stone roof, slapping at them both as if someone, somewhere were trying to get them to part.

It didn't work.

At that moment, Kieran knew there was no power on earth or anywhere else that could have torn him from her.

She shuddered in his arms and then sighed into his mouth when his fingers stroked up her ribs, to the edge of her bra…and then he was under it, pushing the fragile fabric aside to touch the underside of her breast and every cell in his body erupted with need.

"No." Julie abruptly broke their kiss, her breath coming in sharp, staggering gulps. Hair whipping about her face in the wind, she pushed out of his embrace and stood watching him through wide, shocked eyes. "Don't."

Kieran's body was on fire. Hard and hot and ready, he wanted nothing more than to throw her to the stone floor, tear off her clothing and take her. He knew that if he could have her, this connection he shared with her would either broaden or break. And he found he wanted that clarity. This fragile bond that hovered between them, neither strong enough to help him nor weak enough that he could ignore it, was unacceptable.

"You want me. I feel it."

She drew another unsteady breath and laughed shortly, with no humor in the sound. "Yeah. I do. I also want calorie-free chocolate, but I'm not gonna get it."

Kieran shook his head, refusing to be put off. Damn it, he ached for her. Another kiss and she'd be willing to give herself to him. One more kiss. One more touch…

As if she could read his thoughts, though, she took another step back and held up one hand, palm out to ward him off.

"What game are you playing, woman?" His voice was strained, taut with the need still grabbing at his throat. "You're not a child, afraid of her own needs. What keeps you from me?"

"I'm not afraid of *want,* damn it. And this isn't a game." She laughed again, a sharp scrape of sound that held more pain than amusement. "A game. God, I wish it were." Her eyes fired as she shook her head and pointed an accusing finger at him. "You touch me and I see…things. Things that make no sense. Things I shouldn't be able to see."

As if a bucket of cold water had been upended over him, Kieran's desire died in a breath. Fool. He'd been so lost in *her* thoughts, he'd forgotten to protect her from taking too many of *his* memories. Thoughts. Plans.

Regrets.

What had she seen?

How much?

He reached for her, but she shook her head fiercely and skipped back out of his reach. "No. No more touching. No more anything until you tell me…what is going on?"

Her voice broke and Kieran scrubbed one hand across his face in frustration. He'd pushed her too far too quickly—losing himself for a few stolen moments. And now, he would have to deal with the consequences. Grimly he ordered, "Tell me what you saw."

Still shaking her head, she licked her lips, drew in a shaky breath and whispered, "Fighting. A castle made of polished black stone, flashing in the sunlight. Ships. Old ships, with sails. Cannons firing, smoke lifting into the air. The noise." She sucked in a breath. "Tremendous. As men screamed and explosions rattled the air. I saw *knights*." She covered her mouth with one hand as if trying to shove that last word back down her throat. But it was too late.

Lifting her chin, she stared at him and it gave Kieran a pang to see tears glimmering in her emerald eyes. Was there anything harder in the world for a man to take than watching a strong woman cry?

"And I saw *you*." She stopped herself, then said, "No, that's not quite right. I didn't see you. I *was* you. Looking through your eyes. Watching a battle, shouting at men to take cover. Swinging a heavy sword, for God's sake. And then seeing…"

"What?" he asked, his own throat tight as he relived his memories through her eyes.

"A man. Coming out of the smoke and sound. His armor was different. A kind of…crest on the breastplate. And he paid no attention to the battle. He wasn't there to fight. He was there to kill."

"Julie…" His back teeth ground together. His fists clenched at his sides.

She rushed on, her words tumbling from her mouth now, as if she couldn't have stopped them even if she'd wanted to. "He was there to kill you."

She staggered back a step and her eyes widened, a single tear rolling down her cheek, moonlight catching it and making it shine like silver. "Oh my God, he *did* kill you. That sword. Oh God." Her voice broke again, her breath hitched and she clapped both hands to her head as if trying to push the images torturing her away. "I can *feel* it. Feel the edge of the sword. He hit your head first. Slicing. Pain. Staggering pain. Unexpected."

"Julie." His insides opened, and he was half-surprised he couldn't see his guts spilling at his feet. It had been a long time since he'd remembered that day. Since he'd *allowed* himself to remember. It was enough that he kept in mind the lessons learned on the day he died.

"This can't be happening," she whispered, shock, disbelief in her voice. "None of this is real. Can't be. So if it's not real, I'm crazy. Just like him. Is insanity contagious?" She shook her head and kept muttering, just under her breath. "How could I see him die? He's standing right here. That doesn't make sense, damn it."

Her gaze snapped to his and there was misery and accusation shining in her green eyes. "*Nothing* in my life has made sense since you walked into my kitchen. Why is that? Why did you come to my house? Why did you kiss me? Why is this all happening?"

"I can't give you the answers you want," he said softly. "At least, not all of them." Kieran moved toward her, not sure what he should do. Seeing her face, watching her as she experienced his death, so long ago, he knew he would now have to answer at least some of her questions. She had tapped into the deepest well of his soul.

Found the hidden corners where he'd stored away the memories of the day of his death. And now that those images were hanging in the air between them, he felt the old fury rise up inside…fresh as the day it had been born.

It was one thing for *him* to see her thoughts, feelings. It was quite another to know that she had explored his past, experienced the agony he'd kept to himself for so long. He didn't like this at all. Damn it, he didn't want her pity. Didn't need her tears. Was *nothing* sacred?

"Dying didn't bother you," she murmured, obviously unaware of what her words were doing to him. "You were prepared for that. Expected that. It was the *betrayal*. That sliced deeper than the sword. Pain. Pain so sharp. So all-consuming that when he stabbed you through, you didn't even feel it."

"Enough," he said, his voice an angry snarl as his previous attempts at gentle understanding evaporated in an instant. "No more. I won't discuss that with you. A man's death is a private thing."

"Private?" she repeated, clearly stunned. "Your death? Private?"

"It was long ago."

"You died," she said flatly. "Long ago."

"Yes."

Her gaze swept him up and down with a dismissive, angry glance. "You don't look dead."

"It didn't last."

"Right." She laughed again, wild and just touched with hysteria. "Just a tiny death then. Temporary. Or maybe not. Maybe this was…what? A near death experience at Medieval Times?"

"No." He sneered at the mention of the theme restaurant that put waiters and waitresses in the roles of medieval knights and ladies. He and Santos had attended a show there once but had left midway through the "entertainment." There had simply been too many things wrong for them to take any enjoyment from the so-called jousts and combats. The situation was no different from movies that would make Nathan shout at the military inaccuracies portrayed. Every man had his time.

Julie was staring at him as though she half expected him to disappear with a rattle of chains.

Grimly he told her, "I'm no ghost."

"No," she said, rubbing her fingertips over her still bruised lips. "You're way too solid for that. But…"

Kieran sighed, planted his feet in an unconscious stance for combat. Long before he died, he had learned that talking with a woman could make a man long for the clean, uncomplicated rules of a battlefield. Folding his arms over his chest, he stared at her, trying to judge just how much information she could take in without being pushed over the edge into true hysteria.

While he watched her, Julie's eyes hardened, her chin lifted and her back instinctively went poker-straight. There was more going on here than she could ever imagine. That much she knew. She still couldn't believe the images that were burned into her brain, but she knew with a bone-deep certainty that they were all *real*. That somehow, someway, she had tapped into Kieran's mind and seen much more than he had wanted her to see.

But now it was too late. There was no going back. She couldn't *un*-see what she'd already seen. She couldn't forget those images. And she *wouldn't* pretend otherwise.

"You owe me some explanation for all this." She whipped her hair out of her eyes when the wind tossed it across her face. "Damn it, Kieran, what is going on? Tell me. I'm not going to fall apart and I think I've earned the right to some answers."

After a long minute, he solemnly nodded. "You have. I will tell you what I can." He paused again, as if choosing his words carefully. "I have already told you that the killer loose in your city is not a man, but a demon."

He had, but she hadn't believed him. "Yeah, but—"

"And that I am the only one who can capture it."

"Yes…"

The moon dipped behind a bank of clouds and the pale light dimmed, leaving her and Kieran standing together, wrapped in shadows. Julie shivered and clutched the edges of the shirt he'd given her tighter around her.

He blew out a breath, locked his gaze with hers and said softly, "I am a Guardian. One among many."

Steeling herself for the rest of the story, Julie asked, "What exactly is a Guardian?"

"A warrior. In the end, that is all we are." He shifted his gaze from hers to the lights of the city stretching out into the horizon. Walking to the roof's edge, he planted both hands on the battlements and leaned forward, staring off into the night.

"We are given a choice," he said, his voice almost lost in the soft sigh of wind, "at the moment of death. We can choose to remain dead, allow our spirits—our souls—to move on. To go to whatever waits for us…or, we can choose to continue to fight."

"To continue…*how?*" She could hardly believe she'd asked the question. Was she believing this?

Did she really think that Kieran was a long-dead warrior looking for new battles?

He glanced at her over his shoulder and his pale eyes seemed dark, somehow. There was no light there. No warmth. There was only…acceptance. Of his destiny? Of her disbelief?

She couldn't be sure.

"We become Immortals."

"That's impossible."

"Is it?" He spun around to face her, moving so quickly, she hardly saw the movement. Then he leaned one hip against the cold, stone wall and studied her again.

He *looked* like a man who belonged in a castle. His broad, bare chest gleamed in the half-light. His too-long hair whipped in the breeze and his hard eyes were narrowed into slits. "The castle you saw when we kissed. Black stone. Glittering in the sun."

"Yes." She saw it again as clearly as if she'd been born there.

"Edinburgh Castle," he whispered reverently. "A fortress like no other. It looks as though it were clawed out of the stone by the hand of God Himself. Nearby, the sea crashes against the rocks and the ships you saw firing on the castle were *English*." He said that one word with venom. "While my Queen was gone, the English attacked."

"Your Queen?" Julie whispered.

"Mary," he said, straightening up in an instinctive posture of respect, "Queen of Scots."

"Oh, my God…"

He turned from her, stared out over the light-dusted darkness and continued, more to himself than to her. "The battle was fierce. Unexpected. We fought bravely, but the cannonade from the sea defeated us. We couldn't withstand the continuous volleys from the ships."

Julie was lost in the haunted sorrow of his voice. He spoke in an agonized whisper that tore at her heart even as it defied belief.

"I directed the men," he said, his hands now fisting on the cold stone. "We held and the sounds of swords clashing and the ringing of blows on armor was almost like music. Wild, vicious music. And then it was over." His voice hardened, his jaw tightened and his right fist punched the wall as though *it* were the enemy who had once defeated him.

"How is this possible?" she asked, not really expecting an answer.

"An English knight charged through the fallen Scots, kicking their bodies out of his way as he ran to me. I grabbed my sword…" He stared into space, seeing it all again.

Just as Julie was. Her brain replayed the images she'd seen only moments before. She watched the knight charging across bodies, feet sliding in pools of blood that gleamed on the black stone. She saw him lift his sword and bring it down onto Kieran.

She felt Kieran's shock as he blocked that first swipe with the edge of his own sword, his opponent's blade just barely catching the side of his head. Watched him sidestep the first blow only to stagger in shock and pain before falling beneath the second when his attacker shouted "For Madeline!"

"I died that day," he said tightly, turning to look at her, burning his gaze into hers, daring her to not believe. "It was May, in the year of Our Lord, 1573."

Chapter 9

Though her stomach was twisting and turning with the flurry of nerves and confusion rattling there, Julie looked into his eyes and knew that he believed what he was telling her. Truth or not, it was clearly *his* truth.

"I don't even know what to say," she finally admitted and silently added *or think.*

"You need say nothing," he countered and the rigid set of his jaw tightened. "I don't tell you any of this to win your pity. Or your derision—"

"Kieran…"

"Don't deny it," he said, the words clipped, "I can read your disbelief in your eyes. Though you saw it all clearly enough when we kissed."

"I did, you're right." Julie took a step closer to him, drawn by some inexorable need to touch him. She laid one hand on his arm and felt the muscles beneath her palm bunch. "I don't understand how that happens. *Why* it happens. But how can I believe that what you're saying is real? Immortals? Demons? It's like a bad TV series."

Moving with a liquid speed she didn't see coming, Kieran grabbed hold of her waist and pulled her flush against him. His chest was like iron and other parts of his body were just as hard.

"Woman," he said with a tired shake of his head, "you ask for answers and when you get them, you discount them. Hear me now. This is all you need to know. I am a Guardian. I hunt demons that escape their own dimensions through portals into ours. I return them to their hell. It is my duty. It is who and what I am."

The heat of his body slid into hers, driving away any chill brought on by the wind or his words. His strength surrounded her, his eyes demanded she listen. But *believe?* How could she? It was all too fantastic. And yet…

"There are portals between dimensions?" she murmured, wondering why one more unbelievable statement should surprise her at all.

"There are."

"How many?" she asked, hiding her own confusion by falling back on her instincts to gather information. "Dimensions, I mean."

"Infinite," he said and his hands moved on her back, his strong fingers kneading her flesh through the silky material of the shirt he'd loaned her.

"And portals?"

"As many. Or more."

The one problem with asking questions was that sometimes, you didn't like the answers.

"This is too much," she said and heard the tremble in her own voice. Though she could admit, at least to herself, the tremors rocking her had as much to do with his touch as what he was saying. "How can you expect me to believe all of this?"

"Believe or don't. It doesn't matter," he said, looming over her until Julie had to tip her head back just to keep looking into his eyes. His grip on her tightened, holding her to him so closely, Julie could barely draw a breath.

"Then why am I here?" she countered quickly. "If it doesn't matter what I believe, why would you tell me any of this?"

"Because we are 'connected,'" he admitted and he didn't look very happy about it.

"The telepathy thing?"

"Yes."

His hands on her back moved, sliding up and down the length of her spine, kindling fires that burned low and deep. Was he trying to seduce her, soothe her, or *distract* her? All of the above were working. She sighed, closed her eyes and swayed into him.

"So you can't do it with everyone?"

"No."

His thumb and forefinger unhooked her bra with an ease that spoke of experience. She sighed as his hands swept around her back to her front to cup her breasts in his big, warm, palms. *Wow.* Her blood hummed, her body jolted with anticipation. His fingers teased her hard nipples and the sweet sensation shot straight down to her middle.

"Oh, my…" She swallowed hard, shook her head and tried to keep thinking, despite the distraction. *Think, Julie…* But it was so hard to think with his hands on her. "Why can you do it with me?"

Still tormenting her breasts, he dipped his head and tasted her throat. "Stop talking," he muttered, breath dusting her skin.

Lips, teeth, tongue, explored her flesh and sent tendrils of expectation flooding her body. Her brain heated up, thoughts melting as she gave in to the need nearly strangling her. How had she let this happen? How had she allowed herself to be so distracted?

Oh, yeah, she thought as he dipped one hand down, farther, farther, until it slipped beneath the waistband of her jeans, under the thin elastic of her panties and reached down to cup her heat. *That's how.*

She grabbed hold of his shoulders, knowing she should push him away until she had all the answers she needed. But it had been *way* too long since she'd had an orgasm that wasn't centered around her shower massage.

He rubbed the hard core of her center until fireworks exploded behind her eyes. Her knees went weak and she wobbled unsteadily. She moaned softly and moved into his hand, wanting more, wanting him to touch her inside. She held on as if for her life, fingers gripping his bare shoulders tightly. Her head tipped back and his mouth continued its gentle assault.

One hand on her breast, thumb brushing over

her hard nipple again and again, one hand down the front of her jeans, his fingers caressing one small, oh, so sensitive spot.

"Kieran…" She sucked in air as need built and fired within. Spirals of something delicious unwound inside her and she rocked her hips into his hand eagerly.

Every inch of her body was alive and buzzing. Her stomach fisted, her throat tightened as she felt the waves of desire rise higher and higher within. And just as release was so close she could taste it, he slid his hand lower, dipping first one finger and then another into her hot, slick depths.

All she wanted was to strip off her clothes, stretch out on the stone roof and have Kieran's body drive into hers. How could he make her feel all of this with a touch? With a kiss?

How was it possible to *need* so much?

He shifted, lifting his head to look down at her. He moved his hand from her breast to the back of her head. Threading his fingers through her hair, he pulled her head back and watched her eyes as she trembled and shook in his grasp.

"Please," she murmured, seeing him through

a haze of passion that nearly blinded her. "Oh God, please…"

"Come," he ordered, a deep-voiced demand issued through gritted teeth. "Come and let me watch you."

She stared into his eyes, where fires flashed in those pale blue depths. Her thighs parted, her hips lifted, welcoming his touch as his hand stroked her harder, faster. Inside and out, he claimed her, rubbing, caressing, tormenting, pushing her to the edge and finally, finally, *over* that edge.

She shouted his name as her body exploded and as she gasped for air, he took her mouth again, plunging his tongue inside. She met his hunger with a rich new need of her own. She'd never known anything like this before.

As he kissed her, she saw his thoughts again and this time, the images were of *her*. Naked, sprawled across a sumptuous bed, with Kieran atop her, driving his body into hers until they were both breathless.

And even while her body sizzled with an incredible release, a fresh, even stronger desire clamored in its wake.

"That," he said when he finally tore his mouth

from hers in a breathless rush, "is why we are linked. There is a bond between us. A *destined* bond."

"Destined?" she said as he slowly released her and stood her on her own shaky feet.

"Our minds, our bodies. When we join, we strengthen each other." He smoothed her hair back from her face with a surprisingly gentle touch. "I was not looking for you," he admitted, his voice now as quiet as the wind still drifting across the roof. "But you are here and I cannot deny it any longer."

Julie's brain was still buzzing from the force of her climax and here he was trying to have a conversation. For Pete's sake, she couldn't just turn passion on and off like that. But, she was pretty sure she'd heard him clearly. "We strengthen each other?"

"Yes."

"So when I see your thoughts, you see…"

"Yours, yes," he said, then added, "you miss your family. They are too far away and you don't see them as often as you would like."

Julie blinked up at him. True. Her parents and her younger brother were still in Ohio and being apart from them was harder than she had thought it would be. But having him "see" that reality in her mind was disconcerting to say the least.

"I had no family," he said softly, almost wistfully and it caught her off guard.

"No brothers? Sisters?"

"They died as children."

"I'm sorry." What else could she say?

"Times were harder then. Life much shorter."

"In ancient Scotland."

"You believe me?" He asked this with the smallest curve of his lips.

"I'm not sure," Julie admitted. But she'd seen too many of his memories not to be more than halfway convinced. They were clear and sharp images of a long gone time. Images that only a man who had lived them could produce.

"You are…more than I expected," he said and lifted one hand to brush her windblown hair back from her face.

"There is a softness in you that calls to me."

"I'm not a softie," she protested, proud of her innate strength, her ability to take care of herself. To rebound from disaster.

"Softness in a woman is nothing to feel shame over."

"Maybe in *your* world," she said and turned her face into the wind. God, was she really starting to accept that he was more than four hundred years old? Could her mind actually bend far enough to acknowledge that possibility?

And if she did, how much more would she have to accept? "But here," she continued, "if a woman wants to get along, she has to be stronger, harder, faster, smarter than any of the men she works with."

"I'm not a stranger to your time, you know," he said with that all-too-brief smile on his mouth again.

Julie wanted to bite it.

"I have watched as the world changed. And some of those changes are good ones."

"Gee, thanks." Shaking her head, she looked into his eyes and said, "I'm standing here, looking at you, feeling your hand on my cheek and all the time, I *know* this can't be real. I hear you say you've looked into my mind. I know I've seen into yours, but it's impossible."

The frown she knew so much better than his smile reappeared briefly. "You would still try to deny what lies between us?"

"The *destiny* thing you talked about you mean?" Julie sucked in a gulp of cold night air and shifted her gaze to the distant jewel-like lights of the city. "How can I not? I don't believe in destiny," she said tightly. "I believe we make our own choices. Our own fates."

"Then why do I know so much about you?" he countered, gently turning her face with his fingertips until she was looking at him again. "How do I know you love ice cream and hate sushi? I agree with you there, by the way. Raw fish cannot be appetizing. I know that you enjoy cold weather and you hate being hot. That you prefer rainy days to sunshine. That you dream of writing books, but haven't the confidence yet to try."

"Stop," she whispered, as a cold chill tiptoed up her spine. *Too much,* her mind screamed. He knew too much. How could he know all of this? How could he know *her* so well?

"And," he added, "how do I know that the man you thought you loved betrayed you?"

Julie went stiff as a pole.

"You are better off without him."

"Excuse me?"

"Your husband," he said, his voice no more than a soft rumble of sound in the night. "He was a cheat and a liar. He wasn't worthy of you."

"You saw…" Mortified, Julie just stared at him, unsure of just what she could say. Thoughts of Evan flooded her and in a blink of time, she compared him to this man standing in front of her. And Evan came out pretty badly in the comparison.

Kieran MacIntyre was a different kind of man entirely. Strong and sure of himself, he moved through his life with purpose, doing what he considered his duty whether he wanted to or not. Evan had drifted through life, just as he'd drifted through their marriage.

"Your father never liked him," Kieran said, then added, "a wise man."

"Okay, knock it off," Julie countered quickly. "I'm not going to stand here with you prancing through my mind picking out little pieces of my past to talk about."

"I do not prance."

She ignored that and the offended look on his face. "Oh and while we're at it, I don't ever want to talk about my marriage again. Okay?"

"Agreed," he said amiably enough with a nod of his head. "And in return, I ask that you not discuss the day of my death again."

"Deal." God, she had just made one of the weirdest bargains of her life. *You don't brain peep on me and I won't on you.* How the hell was this happening?

"I'll take you back inside now," he said, cupping her elbow with one big hand.

She dug her heels in. "Why?"

"I have to go out."

"To hunt for the demon."

"Yes." He steered her toward the stairs and his strength pretty much ensured her cooperation. "You'll be safe here."

She looked behind her at the darkness surrounding the castle…at the lights from the city… at the half-moon glowing in the sky.

Safe?

Safe from the demon—if there was one— maybe. Safe from Kieran MacIntyre…she wasn't so sure.

Kieran moved through the house riding a wave of irritation and annoyance that was choking him. He hadn't meant to take her like that. To touch her, lose himself in her. Hadn't meant to dip so deeply into her mind that he saw her family, their love for

her and each other. To feel that awareness of
family and to be reminded once more that he
himself had never known such closeness. Such
intimacy.

In more than four hundred years, he had never
allowed himself to become attached to a mortal.
Their lives were too short. To open himself to
friendship, affection, would have invited pain.
And he'd known enough of that in his own lifetime to last him an eternity.

Yet, just an hour ago he'd broken his own code
with Julie Carpenter. And knowing that his power
had grown and strengthened because of it only fed
the rage engulfing him.

Because of what he'd received from their moments in the darkness, even here, in his house, he
could feel the demon's energy signature. So he
knew that his time with Julie was worth whatever
irritation was sparking inside him. If he kept Julie
close, if he allowed himself to develop this connection with her, then the demon would be caught
that much sooner.

Fewer people would die.

As it should be.

And yet...

His boots on the stairs sounded overly loud in the quiet, but he didn't care. The hem of his black leather coat swirled around his knees as he hit the bottom of the staircase and made a sharp turn to head down the long hall.

The familiarity of the place seeped into him, easing the jagged edges of his soul. The gray stone walls, the arched doorways, the portraits of old friends he'd had painted centuries ago. He stalked through the dining room and barely noticed the banquet-size, gleaming walnut table with its centerpiece of dozens of white roses in a pewter urn. The soft light from wall sconces shaped like ancient torches threw shadows on the walls, but these were comfortable shades—ones he usually welcomed. In this house, he had found peace.

Until recently.

He stalked down the hallway, knowing that the one place he could be sure of finding Nathan was in the kitchen. The Navy SEAL was always hungry.

Slamming through the swinging door, he stopped and glared at Nathan, sitting at the table with more of the chicken they'd had for dinner.

"She piss you off already?" he asked, sparing Kieran a quick glance.

"She's none of your concern."

"Destined Mate, huh?" Nathan picked up a chicken leg, leaned back in his chair and took a big bite.

Kieran frowned, remembering that the other man had spoken to Santos earlier. "Santos never could keep his mouth shut."

"Hey, it's just more of the whole Guardian thing for me to learn, right?" Nathan looked amused, a fact that rankled Kieran more than he could say.

"Destined Mates are legend," he ground out, refusing to recall the strength and energy that had poured into his body when he touched Julie so intimately. Just as he refused to consider the increased might he could be gifted with if he and she actually had sex.

"Not the way it looks to me," Nathan commented, then waved the fried chicken for emphasis as he added, "you can damn near see what's between you two when you're in the same room." He chuckled to himself. "Hell, I needed a cigarette myself every time you looked at her."

Kieran scowled at him, but the man was, as always, unintimidated.

"So I'm thinking the legend is more real than any of you guessed. But, I'm not looking to find a woman for eternity. Hell," he added laughing, "the longest I've ever been involved with anyone is a couple months. Eternity? No thanks."

Kieran's thoughts exactly.

But even as his brain agreed, his body hungered for Julie. His hands itched to claim her, his blood pumped for her. And because those desires were strong enough to send him back up the stairs and into her room, he moved for the back door instead. The door that led to the backyard and the ten-car garage beyond.

"Keep watch on her," he said, meeting Nathan's gaze.

"You goin' hunting?"

"Yes."

"Sure you don't want me with you?"

He stopped. "You know the rules. One Guardian to catch one demon. Your time will come."

"No one says you can't have backup."

True. More than once, Guardians had come together over a particularly vicious beast. But in the end, it was the task of a sole man—or woman—to capture the demon.

"It's more important that you stay here. Protect Julie."

Nathan stood lazily and nodded. "Count on it."

Kieran glanced up at the ceiling as if he could see through the house to the bedroom where Julie was staying. Then he shifted his gaze back to Nathan. He didn't want to leave her—which told him it was imperative for him to get some distance from the woman who was quickly becoming far too important to him.

"I *am* counting on it," he said, then walked out the door and slammed it behind him.

Glee.

The bliss of being free to wander a world lush with bodies just waiting to be slaughtered. Who should it pick? How to decide between all the lovelies? The redhead from the movie house still called to him, though a blond woman nearby was equally as tempting.

Still, it had already enjoyed a blond. Variety. The key to enjoying one's work was variety. Leaving the theater, the demon, now disguised as a handsome man with smiling eyes and a neatly trimmed beard stepped up to the redhead. Using the spellbinding energy the gods had gifted it with, it introduced itself. "Hello, my name is Bob Robison. Could I interest you in a cup of coffee?"

She turned and smiled up at it, never seeing it for what it really was. Never realizing that this night would be her last and that before the sun dazzled the sky, she would be screaming for it to end her pain.

Bliss.

Kieran prowled the city, haunting every alley, checking every dirty corner and doorway. He spoke to the denizens of the night, asking questions of the desperate, the lonely, and still was no closer to picking up the demon's trail again.

At the house, he'd been so sure that he would be able to run it to ground tonight. Now, doubt crept through him with the damp stillness of winter fog sliding in off the ocean.

He tasted the air, searching for the scent that would lead him to his prey. He squinted into the neon-lit shadows, hoping for a flash of the energy signature the demon would leave wherever it passed. His footsteps echoed weirdly in the night as he moved quickly down alleyways littered with refuse and the stench of trash and broken dreams.

And when the city gave up none of its secrets, he drove to the hills again. This demon thrived on cities, but craved solitude for its crimes. In the brush and trees of the Hollywood Hills, it could have both. Here is where he would find it—somewhere in the dark canyons filled with shadows large enough to hide all manner of secrets.

Julie was still trembling. A long hot bath in the tub built for orgies hadn't helped. The thick, plush robe she'd found on the back of her bathroom door wasn't doing her any good, either.

She'd made a couple of phone calls—first to check on Kate, who, thank God, was recovering more quickly than the doctors had hoped. And then, she'd called home. Maybe it was hearing Kieran talk about her parents, maybe it was more simple than that—wanting to reach for her touchstone of normality and reason. But even talking to her mom, the most grounded woman on the face of the planet, hadn't soothed the uneasiness rippling within.

Chills crawled through her blood, despite the fact that some parts of her were so hot she could hardly sit still. And because she couldn't settle, she paced around the edges of her room and tried not to think of it as a velvet-lined cage.

But wasn't that all it really was? Kieran Mac-Intyre had swooped into her life, all billowy coat and mesmerizing eyes and nothing would ever be the same again. Here she was, little more than a prisoner in a castle, for God's sake…allowing a man she hardly knew to—

"Oh God." She covered her face with her hands, then scooped them through her hair.

Despite the bone-deep cold racking her, she threw open the French doors and stepped out onto her balcony. It was foolish, she knew, but at least being outside made her feel less locked down. Just an illusion, of course. Because the reality was far less appealing.

She'd allowed herself to be brought here and there was no way out. She didn't know how to get those damn security gates open and she sure as hell couldn't climb them. And even if she *did* find a way through the gates, she didn't have a car and it was a long walk back down into the city.

Oh, yeah, coming here was just a brilliant maneuver.

"Guardians. Demons. *Destiny*."

None of it was true.

Couldn't be.

Her gaze narrowed on the sea of lights spreading out on the horizon. She needed more information. That's what she was good at. Digging into the under layer of what people presented to the world. She'd done a cursory search on Kieran when she'd first met him. Now, though, she needed to go deeper. And while she was at it, she could look into Nathan Hawke.

She had her laptop with her. Kieran had already told her the castle was equipped with wireless Internet service. Castle? Internet? There were two words that so didn't belong in the same sentence.

Yet, what about any of this made sense?

Even if she found nothing, at least she would be doing something. And just looking would hopefully keep her too busy to think about those moments on the roof with Kieran.

She scrubbed her hands up and down her arms as her gaze drifted from the sea of lights on the horizon to the darkness huddled close to the castle walls. There was…*something* out there. Hissing in a breath through gritted teeth, she fought the sensation of eyes watching, measuring, considering.

She wouldn't give in to an unreasonable fear. This was no more than her imagination, stirred by a man with a real gift for it. There was no one out there, in the shadows. No one was watching her.

And yet…

She shivered and backed away from the stone rail. Then, telling herself to get a grip on reality, she turned and with a determined stride, walked back into her bedroom, closed the doors on the night and settled down for some serious investigating.

Her screams still ringing in its ears, the demon laughed, holding its pleasure tightly. It looked down on the redhead's body, empty now, the soul gone into whatever dimension she had been slated for.

It had been right to choose the redhead after all. She had amused him with her frantic, futile battle to free herself. And her blood smelled of ambrosia. The memory was thick and rich and the demon sighed its pleasure. But, the beast still had work. No time to rest on its laurels. There was much to do to prepare the body for the Guardian. And this time, the demon would leave its prize where MacIntyre would be sure to find it.

Humming a little tune, the beast gripped its knife and happily went to work.

The Internet could be a dangerous thing.

Julie leaned back in her chair and tried to catch her breath. It didn't help. "Oh God. Now what?"

An hour ago, she'd typed in Nathan Hawke's name on her favorite search engine. She'd imagined that by quickly finding out that Nathan was as alive as she, she could end all of this. Tell herself none of it was real.

Bad idea.

She glanced at the notepad beside her still-open computer and read the words she'd underlined in thick, black ink.

Nathan Hawke, Navy SEAL, died March 25, 2003.

There had even been a picture of the man in his hometown newspaper obituary. 'Rhode Island man killed in line of duty,' the headline had read and the picture of Nathan could have been taken that afternoon.

Creeped out, but not deterred—or convinced— by any means, Julie had then looked deeper into Kieran's background. Putting aside the whole fact of Nathan being dead, since she had seen him inhaling fried chicken only a few hours ago, she focused on the man who had dragged her into all of this in the first place.

Instead of the cursory search she'd done initially, she called on all of her reporter's skills to peel back the layers of subterfuge that hid the man from the world.

And in the end, she'd found no comfort. Only more questions. More confusion. Now, she looked at the picture staring back at her from her computer screen.

It had been taken in 1955. A group of men gathered around a groundbreaking ceremony for a new children's hospital. The photo was grainy and the focus was terrible, but it made its point anyway.

In the back row of men, Kieran MacIntyre stood just a little apart from everyone else. His pale eyes stared into the camera as if trying to melt it through sheer will. He didn't look happy about being caught on film. And she could understand why.

Anyone else coming across this picture would assume that the man in the photo was Kieran's father and that the resemblance between the two men was simply a startling display of heredity.

But Julie knew better.

She knew that face as well as she knew her own.

And there was only one explanation for its existence.

Everything Kieran had told her was true.

She leaned back in her chair and laid one hand on her suddenly churning stomach. She went back over everything he'd said to her on the roof—about the connection between them. About his duty. Destiny.

About how when they came together, they *strengthened* each other.

Is that why he'd taken her up to the romantic spot on the roof? Why he'd touched her so intimately? Why he'd given her a climax that had left her shaken right to the bone?

To gain strength for his "hunt"?

Julie groaned tightly and realized the real truth at last.

Kieran MacIntyre hadn't brought her here to his house to protect her—but to *use* her.

Chapter 10

Dressed in jeans, her gray sweater and a pair of sneakers, Julie made her way downstairs. This had seemed like a perfectly reasonable plan fifteen minutes ago. Now that she was actually doing it, however, she wasn't so sure.

Her stomach kept spinning and her heartbeat pounded like a wildly shaken maraca. If she accepted the fact that Kieran was what he claimed to be, then she also had to accept the fact that there was a demon out there running around in the city.

And that truthfully scared the holy be-whosis out of her.

But she didn't feel any better in this fortress, either. How could she? Kieran hadn't brought her here for her own safety. He'd brought her here because he believed that being around her would make him stronger.

Well, tough.

She wasn't going to be his Energizer bunny.

She wouldn't stay at a place where she felt like a prisoner.

She needed to think.

And there was only one place in L.A. she *always* went when she needed to be alone. To gather her thoughts, face a problem, make a decision.

Tonight, she needed to do all three.

After all, it's not as though she were acting like some brain-dead heroine in a horror flick and running out to meet the stupid monster. Even if she weren't here at the castle, she'd be connected to Kieran. The way he could get into her mind, she wouldn't really be *alone* anyway. He'd know where she was, no doubt. So she'd probably be just as safe anywhere in the city as she was here. Right? Right.

The trick would be, getting out of this damn castle.

She took another step on the staircase and twisted her head from side to side, half expecting Nathan, the *dead* Navy SEAL to appear out of thin air. Hey, if they weren't really dead, maybe they could turn into mist—or bats. Dear God, she thought, not bats.

But there was no one and she kept going. She'd figured this all out in her room as she hurriedly dressed. A man with the kind of money Kieran had would no doubt have more than one car. And to drive his cars, he had to be able to open those damn gates on the mile-long driveway. Well, people kept garage door openers in their cars. She was willing to bet—actually *was* betting—that the gate remotes would be in the cars, too.

All she had to do was steal one.

A wild burst of semi-hysterical laughter scratched at the base of her throat, trying to escape and her fingers tightened on the cool, smooth banister. So now she was going to become a car thief. Excellent. Good move. And hey, if you're going to steal, be sure to do it from a guy who carries a *sword*.

Just a few short days ago, her life had been boringly normal. Work. Friends. Home.

Tonight, she was trying to escape a castle before a dead guy could catch her.

Oh, no, her life wasn't weird.

At the bottom of the stairs, Julie stopped, held her breath and listened. Except for the unusually loud ticking of a grandfather clock that looked as old as time itself, there was nothing. Pale light washed over the gray stone walls and threw soft shadows on the portraits lining the hallway.

Knowing what she did now, she gave them each a longer look as she passed. Knights. Ladies. Were these Kieran's friends? Family?

No, he didn't have family, he'd said.

And sure, you should believe him, because he's been so honest with you so far! Gritting her teeth, Julie gave herself a mental head slap and kept going, toward the kitchen and the back door. No point trying to slip out the front door. No doubt her guard dog, Nathan, was prepared for that. But maybe, if she could convince the man that she—

"Where you goin'?"

She pulled up short, slapped one hand to her chest and whirled around, all in one motion. Glaring at the tall man staring at her, she snapped, "Just hitting me over the head would have been kinder than going for a 'scare me to death' approach."

Nathan winced a little then shrugged. "Sorry about that. I'm used to moving pretty quiet."

"Congrats," she said, trying to catch her breath and think at the same time. "You get an A plus in stealthy."

He gave her a smile that would have been disarming if she hadn't known that Kieran had no doubt told him to keep an eye on her. *Oh, no. Couldn't risk losing his human battery charger.*

"So…" Nathan said, letting his voice drift off into nothingness.

"I was, uh—" she took a breath and went for the plan she'd hatched a few minutes before "—looking for you."

"Why?"

His eyes were cool and interested, his body poised as if to move into action. Were all warrior types that way? she wondered. She'd noticed that Kieran certainly was. Maybe it was a Guardian thing. And why did she care?

"I thought I saw something out the front windows."

He did move then. Like liquid mercury, sliding effortlessly, he closed the distance between them and stared down at her through suddenly hard eyes. "When? Where?"

"Just now," she lied and blessed the training she'd had as a reporter. "I glanced out the window at the head of the stairs and I swear there was a shadow of…*something,* moving out there."

Not a complete lie after all. She had sensed someone out there watching her when she'd been on her terrace. Of course, it could have been anyone. A neighbor out hiking the hillside, teenagers looking for a place to party, a demon. No. She ended that train of thought instantly. No way was it the demon. But even if it had been, it was probably gone now anyway. And if it wasn't, well, she'd like to see it try to catch her in a fast car.

"Stay here," Nathan said shortly. "I'll go out front, check things out."

"Right," she answered as he turned and slid down the hallway, headed for the front of the house. "You do that."

As soon as he was gone, she turned and bolted for the kitchen and the back door. Guilt curled up inside her at sending Nathan out on a wild-goose chase, but she fought it down. She was doing what she had to do. Besides, the SEAL would probably enjoy himself out prowling through the dark.

Now, if she could just make it to the garage while he was at the front of the castle, she knew she could make her escape before he had a chance to stop her.

She shivered in the cold night air, but ignored

the chill in her blood as she slipped from shadow to shadow, headed for the huge garage. Her steps sounded overly loud in her own ears and she prayed that Guardians or whatever they were, didn't have superhuman hearing along with everything else Kieran had talked about.

Reaching the small door to one side of the massive stone building, Julie grabbed the brass knob and whispered a prayer that it wasn't locked. It turned under her hand and she began to hope that things would go her way. Slipping inside, she walked through into the main garage and as she did, lights flickered on. Motion sensors?

A line of cars of every kind stretched out in front of her. Luxury sedans, sports cars, even a huge all-terrain vehicle that any military guy would have sold his soul for. There were even a couple of world class motorcycles in the far bay, but she paid them no attention.

Rushing to the first car in the lineup, a small, black two-seater sports car that, hopefully, had a lot of muscle under its hood, she grabbed the door handle, whispered a quick, prayer and…opened it. As she'd hoped, the keys were in the ignition and there were two buttons on the dash. She vaguely remembered Kieran hitting one of them as they drove up the mountain, so that was the gate remote. As for the other, it had to be for the garage.

She'd only have a minute or two once she fired up the engine. Dead Nathan would be hot on her heels and she had to be ready to go as soon as the door opened. Taking a breath, Julie swallowed hard, locked the doors and hit the garage door opener. Firing up the engine, she waited only long enough for the wide, steel door to open high enough to allow the car to pass under it before she stepped on the gas.

From the corner of her eye, she saw Nathan sprinting across the yard toward her, but she was already rolling toward the first gate. She hit the button, the metal gates yawned open and she was through them, hurtling down the mountainside into the darkness.

She was free.

For the moment.

Kieran's head lifted and his eyes flashed with fury.

Every sense he possessed hummed in alarm.

Julie had escaped. Damn the woman. He

focused his mind to hers, willing himself into her thoughts and he felt her satisfaction at having out-witted Nathan—who would answer to Kieran for failing in his duty.

Go back, he ordered, forcing her to meet his mind as she tasted freedom. She'd left the castle. Left his protection.

And even while rage bubbled and frothed inside him, he felt almost a flash of pride. She'd gotten past Nathan—no small feat in itself—and had actually stolen one of Kieran's cars. She was far more resourceful than he'd imagined.

Julie ignored his mental summons, and his anger blistered inside him like a raging fire. Seeing through her eyes, watching the images of her surroundings fly past her as she pushed the car to its limits, he saw exactly where she was. She was already down the mountain, heading for the freeway.

How had she escaped Nathan?

Why would she want to escape?

He'd thought they'd reached an understanding on the roof. Thought she'd believed him when he told her about the dangers surrounding her.

Woman, he whispered into her mind, *you try my patience.*

He thought he felt her laugh wildly, but then she was gone as if in her own turmoil and emotional state, she'd found a way to block him.

"Damn it," he muttered, as he started down the dirt and brush covered hill. He should have mated with her. Should have forged the link that was already building between them into something more solid.

It was his own fault. He'd hesitated about using her.

Because somewhere inside him, he was concerned that there was more to what he was feeling for Julie than he wanted to admit. She haunted him. Her voice. Her eyes. Her mind.

He dipped into her thoughts and felt what it was to be *alive*. To know love, joy, pain. The tumult of her mind, the richness of her soul was irresistible to a man who'd lived centuries with nothing but his own emptiness for company.

Moonlight poked through the layer of clouds and shadows slanted in long, wavering shapes on the ground in front of him. As if from a great distance, the tickle of some other mind brushed against his and Kieran slid to a stop, sending pebbles and dirt cascading down the hill in front of him.

The demon.

Its thoughts were hardly more than a whisper, but they were there. Excitement. Pleasure. Glory. They all rolled through Kieran like an oil spill sliding across the surface of the ocean.

He scented the air in response, though every cell in his body told him the demon was far away now. There was no hint of it now. No wash of color, no electrical charge in the air. But the demon had made its point. As Kieran's strength grew, so did the demon's. The longer it survived in this dimension, the stronger it would get.

Gritting his teeth against the anger roaring through him, Kieran started down the hill again, determined to reach Julie quickly. He stalked through the shadows, becoming a part of the night that surrounded him. At the foot of the hill, he turned sharply and loped up the road to where he'd left his car.

The scent hit him first.

Fresh blood.

Drawing his sword, he approached the car as no more than the hint of movement. But there was no need for obfuscation. No need to be silent. To creep up on his prey.

The prey had been here and gone.

Stretched across the hood of Kieran's car was what had once been a tall, pretty, redheaded woman. Naked, her body had been sliced open, her organs piled neatly on the dirt before his car. Her wide, surprised eyes stared up at the black sky as if she were wondering how she'd come to meet this end.

Kieran knew.

Just as he knew that if he didn't find the demon, more women would be gutted and left as monuments to its deviance.

"Forgive me," he murmured as he lifted the woman from his car and gently laid her out on the cold, hard asphalt. He didn't want to leave her here, alone, for the coyotes to find, but he had no choice.

He had to get to Julie.

The Santa Monica Pier was crowded, as always.

Neon lights clashed brightly, sending out waves of color to flash over the faces of the people moving up and down the length of the pier. Music spilled from one of the restaurants, mimes in white face paint annoyed the pedestrians and though the carousel was quiet in the night, lights blazed from the Ferris wheel and laughter floated on the ocean-scented wind.

Arcade games whirled, beeped and clanged as people tossed coins, shot at ducks and slapped pinball machines. Teenagers cruised the boardwalk looking for trouble and the fishermen staggered along the railings ignored it all and concentrated on their catch.

A strange place to come when she needed to be alone, Julie knew. But she'd found the pier not long after moving to L.A. and somehow, the carnival atmosphere, the anonymous crowds of people, all came together to provide a sort of white noise. She could be alone with her thoughts while surrounded with the life of the city and somehow she didn't feel as solitary.

The scents of steaming hot dogs, cinnamon flavored Churros and the cloying sweetness of cotton candy mingled in the air and she breathed deep. This at least was normal. This she could understand.

It was the rest of her life that was out of control.

L.A.P.D. had a station right in the middle of the pier and knowing that made Julie feel a little better about being here in spite of Kieran's warnings. She was perfectly safe. Here in this mass of people, she was only one more face in the crowd. That wasn't what he thought, of course. She knew he was furious, but damn it, so was she.

He'd been using her.

Despite what she felt when they were together, despite the heat in his touch and the surge of desire and need she felt coming from him...he was only using her.

And with that ugly thought uppermost in her mind, she took the steps, walked down to the sand and followed the sound of the waves to the very edge of the ocean. Lacy ruffles of water raced to shore, then slid back silently into the black. The tide was out and the wet sand glistened in the moonlight.

Above her, the pier rocked with noise and people. Here on the beach, there were only one or two people walking along the shore. And not too far away, two people cuddled together as they watched the water.

A quick sigh of envy washed through Julie as she turned her gaze back to the expanse of black water shimmering under a partially hidden moon.

Since Evan, Julie had promised herself to guard

her heart. To not let anyone too close. Yet somehow, in spite of everything…the danger, the fear, the worry, the impossible truth of Kieran's existence, she *had* let him get close.

Too much had happened too quickly.

She needed to be able to breathe. To let her mind roam without fear of Kieran picking up on every one of her thoughts. Jamming her hands into her jeans pockets, she kicked at the wet sand, sending a huge clump into the receding water.

She'd felt his anger as she left the castle. Felt his mind enter hers as she drove onto the freeway for the short ride to the beach and she hadn't been able to stop it. Just as she'd guessed, he'd known exactly where she was. But since then, she'd felt nothing. So maybe she was safe here. Maybe he'd lost her trail or whatever.

But even as she thought it, something changed. She felt the shift in the atmosphere as clearly as if someone had tapped her on the shoulder. Kieran? She glanced around, her gaze sweeping the nearly empty beach—yet she saw nothing that hadn't been there a moment ago.

There was no tall, furious man in a long black coat stalking toward her.

She hunched her shoulders anyway, as though in defense against whomever—or whatever—was watching her.

"Woman, you test my patience."

Julie jolted and spun around, staring directly into Kieran's pale blue, furious gaze.

Relief battled with fear and finally won out. Obviously the presence she'd felt watching her had been *him*. Reaching out, she planted both hands on his broad chest and gave him a hard shove that didn't rock him a single inch.

"You scared me half to death. How did you sneak up on me like that, anyway?"

"That is not the question. The question," he ground out, "is why would you leave my home when I told you to stay?"

"Because I don't take orders?" she offered.

"You're a fool," he said tightly and his mouth flattened into a firm line of disapproval.

"And you're a liar," she countered, backing away from him, sliding in the wet sand. Stabbing one finger in the air, she continued, "You didn't take me to your place to protect me. You wanted to use me. You're no better than my ex-husband. You only want me there because you need me to get stronger."

"You believe me. Everything I've told you."

"Oh, you betcha," she said, sliding her hands back into her pockets and fisting them helplessly. "I believe you're just what you say you are. I believe Nathan is as dead as you and I believe that letting you anywhere near me in the first place was possibly the biggest mistake of my life. But thankfully," she added as she started past him, suddenly determined to get away, "that's a mistake I can correct."

He grabbed her arm, spun her around and yanked her close. "You will not leave."

"You can't stop me."

His features looked tight, his eyes were narrowed and his jaw was like iron. "Do not doubt it for an instant."

"I'll run again—the first chance I get."

"No, you won't."

"Damn it, Kieran, I won't be what you want," she cried, her voice lost in the pulse of the sea. "I want my life back. I want to forget any of this happened. I want—"

"Me," he finished for her and took her mouth in a kiss that seared every nerve ending in her body in one hot flash of fire.

God help her, he was right. She did want him. Had from that first moment when he'd surprised her in her kitchen. Seemed like weeks ago, so much had happened since that night and yet, through it all, he had been there. Constantly. In her mind. In her soul. She felt his presence more deeply than anything she'd ever known before.

Maybe she hadn't been fighting him so much as she'd been fighting her own reaction to him. And if that was the case, then she was through doing battle.

Her tongue joined his, resistance forgotten in the rush of heat and sensation pouring through her. His hands swept under her shirt, covering her bare breasts, pulling at her hard nipples until she felt an orgasm building instantly inside her.

She groaned, leaned into him, pulled her hands from her pockets and wrapped her arms around his neck.

Yield to me.

And you to me, she said, whispering into his mind as he had to hers.

Destiny, he murmured, the one word echoing over and over again in her mind, coating her thoughts, dissolving any reservations, clouding all but her need.

A surge of energy rippled around them like an electrical arc. Julie pulled her mouth free of his and looked around them as the air hummed and the world beyond the two of them blurred. "What was that?"

"We are hidden," he whispered, pulling her close to lay his mouth against the curve of her neck. "No one can see us." Lips, teeth and tongue worked her flesh until she shivered with an unbelievable want that built to a crescendo of sensation within her.

Her skin flashed, her insides burned.

His hands took her, lifting her sweater up and over her head, tossing it to the sand. And in the bubble of air surrounding them, she felt no cold. No chill of the night. All she could feel was *Kieran*.

"I must have you," he whispered. "I have tried to keep myself from you, but the need is too great. The hunger too fierce."

"I want you, too." She caught his face in her hands and looked hard at him. "I didn't want to. You should know that."

He leaned in and nibbled at her bottom lip.

She sucked in air hungrily, greedily. "But you touch something in me, Kieran. Something I didn't know I even had. And even though this is probably a huge mistake, all I want is you. Now," she muttered, sliding her hands under his coat, pushing it off his shoulders. Then her fingers moved to the buttons of his black silk shirt and impatient, she ripped the fabric, scattering the shiny black buttons onto the sand.

Everything she'd been feeling, everything she'd been trying to tell herself about staying away, keeping her distance, fell to the side. At that moment, all she could think of was Kieran. His touch. His taste. The feel of his hands and mouth on her skin.

She didn't care if it was destined.

Didn't care if being with him would only pull her deeper into a darkness she didn't totally understand. She knew that if she didn't have him in the next few minutes, feel his body pumping into hers, she would wither and die from the lack of him.

Moonlight played on his skin, making it gleam like old bronze. His eyes flashed and the color deepened from the pale blue she knew so well to a burnished shade of silver that seemed to slice at her insides.

He went to one knee, took her nipples into his

mouth, one after the other and she swayed into him, arching her body, offering more of herself up to him. His tongue and teeth nibbled and licked at her and when he suckled, it felt as though he were drinking deep of her soul, pulling it out of her to rest inside him.

And she wanted more.

People drifted past them, taking the boardwalk steps, walking to the ocean, strolling across the sand and Julie and Kieran might as well have been on another planet. They were hidden in plain sight and the thought of making love in public was so erotic, Julie moaned and held Kieran's head to her breast more tightly.

His hands were busy, unbuttoning her jeans, pulling them down and off, tossing her shoes to one side, then sliding back up the length of her legs, his fingers scraped along her skin. Every nerve in her body was alive. Everything inside her jumped eagerly, awaiting his next touch. And when he moved to slide his fingers into her slick, wet heat, she opened her legs for him, welcoming the fire.

He shifted to cover the bud of her desire with his lips and while he teased that small hard core of her with his tongue, he pushed his fingers in and out of her depths, stroking, beguiling, demanding.

The sounds of the boardwalk rumbled in the distance, discordant music, laughter, the jangle of bells. But here, beneath the pier, there was only Kieran. She threw her head back and shouted his name as the first orgasm crashed over her with the force of a tidal wave, rocking the ground beneath her feet and the very foundations of everything she'd ever believed in.

And before the first tremors were finished, Kieran bent to spread his coat over the sand, then laid her down atop it, pulled off the rest of his clothes and levered himself above her. The head of his shaft paused at her opening and he looked down at her, as if waiting for her to give him leave to enter.

Julie lifted her hips in open invitation, then stretched out, encircling his neck with her arms, pulling his head to hers for a kiss she wanted more than another breath.

He groaned and took what she offered. His tongue tangled with hers, his breath entered her lungs as his body entered her depths.

He filled her with his thick, hard body and she

opened wider, accommodating him even as her hips rocked rhythmically in an ancient dance of need and desire. He plunged into her again and again, as his mouth fed on hers. Their bodies moved together in the moonlight, and there was a music to their mating.

A hum of acceptance.

Destiny.

Julie's soul ached and her body ripened under his invasion. She tightened, expectation sliding through her as he pushed her higher and higher, every stroke a caress, every caress a promise of more.

His body was hot and hard. Muscles in his back bunched and rippled as he moved within her. He lifted his head and those silvery eyes looked into hers as the first wave of completion hovered near. She couldn't look away. Couldn't tear her gaze from his any more than she could get up and run from what she was experiencing.

Then she felt him in her mind, murmuring erotic enticements, wild and dark words that tumbled through her with abandon.

Come, Julie. Let go and come. Take me into your heat, hold me there and let me feel your tremors.

Pressure built and built inside her, she couldn't breathe and didn't care. Couldn't move and didn't need to. All she needed, all she could ever want, was Kieran and what he could do to her.

He took her up and up, pushing her body higher and faster than it had ever gone before and when the waiting was too much, when her need was greater than her want, he took her over the edge of sanity.

When she shouted his name on the crest of her release, Kieran finally allowed himself to follow.

Chapter 11

Kieran's head dropped to her breasts as he struggled for air. He felt drained, sated and yet his body was already growing and hardening within her velvety heat again. In centuries of living he'd never known anything like this. Going up on his elbows, he stared down at her as if he'd never seen her before.

And in a way, he hadn't.

He'd known her only as the woman who opposed him at every turn. As the woman who might or might not be his Mate.

But now, he knew. There could be no more doubts. Becoming one with her had opened up new worlds for him. He felt staggered by the raw strength and power coursing through his veins. His body seemed alive in a way it hadn't been in centuries.

His mind was still connected to hers and Kieran gasped as new and wondrous feelings raced through his mind. He felt her joy and shared it, saw explosions of color through her eyes and lost himself in them. Felt her body's reaction to his and sensed her renewed arousal.

The bonds of connection swirled in the air around them, hovering close, ready to tighten and he couldn't fight them. Didn't want to.

His body nearly vibrated with the newness of what he was experiencing. No one had ever told him that finding a Destined Mate would be like this.

But even if they had, he wouldn't have believed. Wouldn't have wanted it.

Now, he couldn't imagine the coming centuries without it.

She struggled for air and a soft smile curved her mouth as she reached up, combed her fingers through his hair and whispered, "That was incredible."

"It was," he said, dipping his head to take a kiss, then another.

"I felt what you were feeling," she said, licking her lips, taking another slow, shuddering breath. "I saw myself through your eyes. Experienced the slide of your body into mine. I actually felt my climax *and* yours. How is that possible?"

"We are joined," he murmured and rocked his hips into hers.

"Joined," she repeated and swallowed hard. Kieran sensed her trepidation and knew when she gave up the worry that would niggle at her later. Knew when she gave herself up to the expectation that was already flowering inside her.

She tipped her head back, her neck curved, her lips parted and a soft sigh slid from her throat. "This is amazing, Kieran. I hear your voice in my head. I *sense* what you're feeling." Her eyes opened and locked on his as a wicked smile danced briefly over her face. "Oh. My. Goodness."

Kieran bent low and licked the long line of her slender neck, tasting her skin, nibbling at her flesh as his body filled hers again. "Your desire feeds me," he muttered, his breath dancing across her skin like a caress. "Your body melds with mine and we become one."

Her body welcomed him, her mind opened for him, showing him all he'd missed for centuries. He reveled in the rush of sensations, gloried in the flow of her knowledge and experiences that filled his mind with all she'd experienced and felt in her life. And when he thought he couldn't feel any more, another layer of his solitude peeled away to be eased by all that she was.

Kieran embraced it all and sought more, like a man whose thirst was so bone-deep he couldn't get enough water. But he would never have enough. Never be able to go deeply enough inside her. Never know enough about her. For all his size and strength, for all his power and knowledge, he knew that he would always want more than he could have of her.

"Kieran," she whispered, lifting both legs to wrap them around his hips and pull him closer, deeper. "I can see you. See all of you. All of the years. The hurts. The pain."

He caught her hand as she cupped his cheek and just for a moment, turned his face into her palm, shame rippling through him. He didn't want her to know all that he'd done in the name of duty. All those he'd killed in battle, all those he'd injured in the name of the hunts that had become all he knew. But he could no more stop her from entering his mind than he could prevent himself from entering hers.

Her thumb stroked his cheek and that simple caress touched him more deeply than anything he'd ever known before. The dark, jagged corners of his soul were soothed and eased, old pains fading away and Kieran had to fight to hold on to his sense of control.

"I want you so much," she whispered, hands sweeping up and down his bare back, fingernails scraping his skin as she arched into him again and again, demanding all he had to give.

She was small and tight and hot. Her bones felt fragile beneath him and he was mindful that a man his size could injure her without meaning to.

He *needed* as he'd never needed before. Every cell in his body, every nerve, every muscle, was strained to the breaking point as he moved within her slowly, keeping a tight rein on the urge to take her hard and fast, to feel her heart beating and her body bowing to his.

Gritting his teeth, he hissed in air, shifted to take hold of her hips and held her still while he moved within her. He was so close, so dangerously close to the edge, he needed to gather all the strength he possessed to hold himself back.

But then she lifted her head and stared into his gaze, desire flashing in her sharp green eyes. "Kieran, I'm not fragile. You won't hurt me." She

pushed her body down onto his, grinding her hips
as he tried to hold her in place. "Don't be gentle.
Take me fast and hard. Make me scream, Kieran.
Make me scream."

Groaning, he grabbed her up off of his coat, sat
back on his heels and held her pinned to his lap. His
fingers dug into her skin as his body speared hard
and high inside her. She twisted in his grasp, clinging
to him, tearing at his shoulders, his hair, taking his
mouth with hers and tangling her tongue with his.

Outside their bubble of secrecy, the wind
howled, clouds scudded across the black sky and
the moon shone fitfully onto an ocean that began
to roil in the wind.

He took her breath and muffled her cries with
his mouth as he pushed them both as high as they
could go. His mind opened wider as his body
erupted into hers. He felt everything she felt.
Knew everything there was to know about her.
And he knew that the same thing was happening
to her. He could shield her from nothing, had no
choice but to share with her as completely as she
did with him.

Her body shuddered and he tore his mouth from
hers, bent his head and took one hard, pebbly

nipple into his mouth. Teeth and tongue tormented her, suckling, nibbling, licking. She moved on him like a wild woman, demanding, taking, giving, and he silently thanked whatever fates had sent her to him.

And in the instant when their bodies exploded simultaneously, Kieran felt the threads of Destiny swirl around them, binding them together for the rest of time.

Something new.

The beast tasted the wind and felt a shift in the balance.

Smiling, it reached out with its mind, found the source and responded.

As they dressed in silence, Kieran sensed Julie's unease. Now that their passion was spent, there were questions bubbling in her mind. Questions he didn't know if he could answer.

"This is such a cliché," Julie said quietly as she lifted her gaze to meet his, "but we really do need to talk."

Scowling, Kieran picked up his coat, shook the sand from its folds, then slipped into it. "Why do

you need to ask me anything? You have already
seen the answers in my mind."

"Seeing them is one thing," she said, pushing
her hair back from her face, "understanding them
is something else."

"Julie—" He stopped speaking, narrowed his
eyes and held up one hand to silence her.

"What?"

He frowned at her. "Quiet. There is something
here. Something…"

"The demon." Julie spun in a slow circle,
scanning the nearly empty beach. "It's here?"

"Yes." Picking up the sword he had thrown to
the sand earlier, he fisted it in his right hand, gave
her one long, hard look and said, "You will stay
here. Do not try to move. Do not speak."

Julie's eyes widened and her jaw dropped.
"You're *leaving* me here? *Alone?*"

"You will be safe." He reached out, laid one
heavy hand on her shoulder and despite the
sudden threat of danger, she felt a quickening of
her pulse at his touch. "We have mated. You share
my energy and so the cloak of secrecy I forged
will remain with you. As long as you stay here."

She nodded, not really trusting herself to speak

at the moment. Her throat was tight and a cold ball of fear settled in the pit of her stomach.

As if their bond suddenly tightened between them, Kieran looked into her eyes, read her uneasiness and reached out to touch her cheek. "I will keep you safe. I swear it."

Julie drew in one shaky breath and managed to say, "Who keeps *you* safe, Kieran?"

His eyes shuttered, the pale blue color suddenly filling with shadows. "Stay."

He left her then and Julie watched from the shelter of secrecy he'd left behind. And even following his movements, she had a hard time keeping track of him. He seemed to become a part of the night. One more shadow in a sea of them. He moved with a liquid grace and deadly strength that left her shivering with both fear and a weird sense of pride.

Moonlight swam over the beach with a silvery glow that only defined the long spears of darkness stretching out from beneath the pier. The ocean's soft, murmuring roar as it lapped at the shore became another heartbeat, pulsing just beneath the rush of sound from the boardwalk above.

She wrapped her arms around her middle and

hung on tightly, straining to keep Kieran in sight. And as she waited, Julie realized just how deep the hole she'd dug for herself really was.

She was *bonded* to a man who really didn't want her for himself—only for the strength she could give him. A demon of all things had apparently targeted her *because* of her link to Kieran. And worst of all, she was falling in love with her sword-carrying warrior.

And what woman wouldn't? The old pain in his eyes urged her to ease it. The aching solitude that he'd experienced for centuries still resonated inside her. He supported countless charities with his staggering wealth and yet never accepted any of the accolades most men would demand. He had spent countless years doing battle with all kinds of evil in an effort to keep the mortal world, that knew nothing about him, safe.

He was unlike anyone else she'd ever known and—

Someone new, a voice, not Kieran's, whispered to her mind. *A surprise for me. The Guardian's lady. How sublime.*

Julie started, cold sweeping through her system as she turned, trying to focus, trying to figure out where the voice was coming from. Who was trying to reach her?

See me soon, the voice promised.

"Kieran!" She screamed for him, her voice raw, scraping against her throat as she shrieked his name over and over again, giving in to the shuddering fear that iced her veins and set her heart pounding.

He was with her in an instant and she flew into his arms, greedily accepting his solid strength, his warmth and the feel of one of his arms closing around her like a vise. In the other hand he held his sword, ready for whatever came their way.

"What is it?" he demanded, holding her tightly while his gaze scanned the area.

"The demon." She shook her head and buried her face in the curve of his neck. Her voice was muffled, but she couldn't seem to help it. "It was in my mind. I thought at first, it was you, but then the feel of it was wrong. Like something evil crawled over me. Cold, Kieran. I'm so cold."

He sheathed his sword even as his mind searched the area. The demon wasn't close. If it had been, it was gone now. But the knowledge that it had reached out to Julie left Kieran more shaken than he would have thought. He hadn't expected that the demon would be able to invade Julie's mind and the fact that it obviously could, would make this hunt all the more deadly.

He must keep her safe. And he must find the beast before *it* found Julie.

"And Nathan lives?" Santos's voice, as clear through the satellite phone as if he were in the room with Kieran, sounded surprised.

"I didn't have to say anything to him," Kieran admitted, disgusted. "His own guilt has punished him more than I could."

In fact, the Navy SEAL had been so furious that a woman—a civilian at that—had outsmarted him, tricked him into letting her escape, he'd locked himself into the castle's gym and was even now doing his best to destroy the equipment.

"His pride is shaken. He'll recover."

"Don't know if I will," Kieran muttered and blurted out the truth that had him more worried than he wanted to admit. "The demon linked with Julie's mind."

A long, silent, thoughtful pause and then Santos's voice came, a low growl of concern. "How is this possible?"

"I don't know." Striding around the perimeter of his favorite room in the castle, the library, Kieran didn't even notice the floor to ceiling bookshelves, the burgundy leather armchairs and couches, the soft lighting glancing off the cut crystal bottles of liquor.

He shoved one hand through his hair and kept talking, voicing the thoughts that had plagued him for hours. "This demon is telepathic," he said tightly, "so maybe when Julie and I—" He stopped talking.

"You bonded?" Santos couldn't have sounded more shocked if Kieran had said he'd sprouted wings and learned to fly.

"Yes." And he was still dealing with the repercussions of that himself. Knowing that by bonding with Julie he might very well have put her in even more danger was just one more thing to be troubled about.

Santos chuckled and Kieran scowled fiercely at the satellite phone.

"Ah, my friend, I would never have thought that you would be the first of us to slip into a bridle and chain."

"There are no bridles. No chains." He wouldn't allow there to be any. "I did what I had to do to capture this demon."

"I understand," Santos said and damned if Kieran couldn't hear the humor in his voice, "you sacrificed yourself for your duty. Very courageous of you my friend."

"Spaniard, you walk a fine line."

"Always, Kieran. It is what makes eternity interesting."

"It's more interesting than it should be around here."

Kieran stopped in front of a pane of glass and stared out into the night. Julie was upstairs in her room and he knew, because he could feel it, that she was still terrified by the demon's intrusion on her thoughts.

"Is your new Mate willing to help you capture the beast?"

Kieran stiffened at the mere thought of allowing Julie anywhere near the demon. "She will be no part of the hunt."

"So you do care for her."

Disgusted, Kieran snapped, "Why do I call you only to be irritated?"

"Because, my friend, you need me to tell you the truths you don't want to acknowledge for yourself."

Kieran slapped one hand to the cold glass and

stared out at the night beyond. "I don't want her in my life, Santos."

"That is unfortunate," Santos said softly, "for both of you."

"Yes. It is," Kieran said and hung up, still staring into the night but seeing instead Julie's eyes when his body entered hers.

Hunger reared up inside him again and he experienced a need so fierce it was as if he hadn't touched her. Hadn't had her in and around him only an hour before. He was a man possessed and damned if he could find a way to regret it.

Julie couldn't sleep. Couldn't seem to sit still long enough to rest. Couldn't even think without wondering if Kieran was hearing her thoughts, feeling what she was feeling, sensing her anxiety.

The night crouched outside the French doors, and she wondered if the demon was out there, waiting for an opportunity to attack her again. Fear fisted in her stomach and she hated herself for being so scared. Hated feeling as though she had to hide. Hated knowing that some nameless beast was determining how she lived her life.

As if to prove to herself that she wasn't afraid,

she walked to the terrace doors and deliberately flung them open. The cold night air rushed in as if it had been perched on the stone floor, just waiting for its chance to pounce.

She shivered, despite the thick robe she wore and knew it was the fear as much as the cold that was racking her body with chills. Taking a few long, deep breaths, Julie stepped forward, easing her way onto the terrace, forcing herself to move when all she really wanted to do was go hide under the bed.

The stones felt cold and rough against her bare feet and her knees wobbled a little as she took another step and then another, moving inexorably to the gray stone railing. Her fingers grabbed hold of that railing and dug in, as if that grip meant her life.

Or at least, her sanity.

Kieran. She thought his name, and the want she felt colored the call.

Closing her eyes, she opened her mind for him, even though a part of her feared the demon would reappear, sliding through her thoughts like black silk, easing into every crevice of her being until—

"Don't."

She turned her head as Kieran approached behind her. "You heard me."

Yes. One word, reassurance and promise.

"I needed you," Julie admitted, turning her back on the night and the city lights in the distance. A sigh of wind drifted over her and she hunched deeper into the folds of her luxurious robe.

"I need you as well," Kieran said, stepping out onto the terrace to take her hands in his and guide her back into the warmth of her room. "But don't risk reaching for my mind, Julie. Don't allow the beast an opportunity."

"I had to see if it was going to do it again."

"I won't allow it."

"Can you stop it?" she asked, watching him as he stepped past her to close and secure the French doors.

"I will find a way," he assured her, turning back to face her again. "The beast cannot get into the castle. It cannot take over an unwilling body."

She drew a slow, deep breath. "But it can kill me."

"*No.*" He moved to hold her, wrapping her in his arms and pinning her to him. "It will *not*. You will be safe, I swear it on my life."

Her heart thudded in her chest. Her stomach spun and twisted and her blood thickened until it ran like sweet, hot honey through her veins. There was so much more she should ask him. So much more she should know. Yet now, all she could think of was being with him. Having him bury his body inside hers.

She pushed out of his arms, untied the cloth belt at her waist and shrugged out of her robe. She watched his eyes flash that burnished silver again and *felt* his desire pumping through his body.

"You are a temptation I cannot seem to resist."

"I'm glad to hear it," she said, stepping up to him again, going up on her toes to wrap her arms around his neck and hang on. "Don't resist, Kieran. I need you inside me. I need your warmth. Your strength. Don't keep them from me."

He growled low in his throat and walked forward, until the backs of her knees hit the edge of the mattress. Then he bent her back and uncoiled her arms from his neck. She reached for him, but he shook his head and tore off his shirt. His gaze never left hers as he quickly stripped, then came back to her.

Scooping his hands under her butt, he lifted

her off the bed, her long legs dangling, feet unable to find purchase.

"Kieran…" Breathless, Julie hung suspended in his grip and met his hungry gaze with a fresh, hot hunger of her own.

"Give yourself to me, Julie," he whispered as he bent his head to cover her center with his mouth.

She gasped, shivered and sighed, then clenched her fists into the silky duvet beneath her naked body. His mouth worked her most intimate folds. Lips and tongue teased and tormented her, swirling, tasting, licking.

Incredible, overpowering sensations washed through her in wave after wave of devastating yearning. It was too much and not nearly enough. Time stood still and yet raced forward, dragging her with it. Expectation coiled deep within her, tightening, tightening, until she thought she would lose her mind and then, finally, her release crashed through her, leaving her weak and trembling and so overcome, tears stung the backs of her eyes.

Then Kieran was there, laying her down, covering her body with his. His pale blue eyes flashed silver as they had before and she recognized the passion flaring inside him.

She smiled up at him, reaching for him even as those so-familiar eyes darkened, shifted into those of a stranger. Fear blossomed inside her as his dazzling, shining, silver eyes became something different. Something terrifying.

His eyes were now empty, black fathomless depths that swallowed her reflection.

Julie tried to scoot out from under him, but his strength held her pinned to the mattress as his features altered, his expression changing, becoming someone she didn't even know. His hard, strong body tightened and pushed into hers. He smiled down at her and his mind touched hers briefly with a darkness she'd never sensed there before.

It was back.

And inside Kieran.

Chapter 12

I have you...

That dark, insidious voice slid through her mind, dripping with evil, with the promise of pain and even her soul cringed.

"No!" She shouted the single word as she tried to buck his much heavier body off of hers. But the action was as useless as trying to single-handedly lift a car. She wouldn't win in a physical contest. Her only chance was to reach the heart of the man she knew. "Kieran!"

Julie slapped at his shoulders, grabbed his thick, black hair with both hands and yanked. She stared up into those empty black eyes and fought the shudder of revulsion swimming inside her. She had to reach him. Had to bring him back and banish the demon.

"Kieran, fight it! Come back to me. Come back now!"

His features shifted, morphing again as she watched, his eyes glazed, lightened and he shook his head as if trying to wake from a deep sleep. His body still pinned hers to the mattress, but this wasn't lovemaking, this was about power.

Brutal strength.

Domination.

Moonlight glittered in the room, a pale wash of color that couldn't even touch the shadows crouching near.

Her heels drummed against his backside as she forced herself to look into his eyes. Her mind reached for his. She was so new at this. So completely unused to trying to reach anyone telepathically, that she was desperately afraid she would only connect with the demon infiltrating Kieran's mind.

But she had to try.

Hear me, Kieran. Her mind focused, she met his gaze, burying the fear within, focusing only on the need to bring him back. *You're with me. With Julie. Come back, Kieran. Come back now.*

His eyes closed, his jaw clenched and his grip on her body tightened until she felt as though he was going to snap the bones in her upper arms. And still she tried.

Kieran, you have to hear me. You have to come back to me.

Heartrending seconds ticked past and she knew both her own and Kieran's lives hung in the balance. *Please come back, Kieran. Fight this thing. Stay with me. Keep me safe.*

That last thought she'd sent him purposely. She knew the warrior in him would respond to the plea for help. To protect her. Then she held her breath and prayed as she never had before.

Julie?

"Oh, thank God," she whispered as she watched the darkness recede from his eyes, leaving only the pale, icy blue she knew so well.

Instantly he released her and in the next moment, he was pulling his body free of hers and leaping off the bed as if he couldn't trust himself to be near her any longer.

Chills racked her and she grabbed at the duvet beneath her, pulling it up and over her bare shoulders. She scooted off the bed, but kept a wary distance between them just in case that other presence was still close.

"Are you…"

His head snapped up and his gaze speared into hers. "Yes, it's me."

She knew that just by looking at him. His own soul shone from his eyes now and the swirl of darkness was gone as if it had never been. But that didn't explain what had happened…or *how* it had happened.

"What was that?" she asked, her fingers clutching at the duvet as she moved across her bedroom and turned on one of the Tiffany lamps sitting on the bedside tables. The stained glass lampshade threw a kaleidoscope of soft blues and greens and reds across the bed and onto the floor.

Kieran's breath huffed in and out of his chest as he stood naked in front of her. As clearly as if he'd spoken of it, she felt his shame and fury arcing around him like lightning in a flashing summer storm.

"Did I hurt you?" he asked and she knew just what it cost him to have to ask.

"No," she said, quick to assure him despite the fact that what had just happened had left her insides quaking. "You didn't. And if you had, it wouldn't have been *you*."

His gaze narrowed on her, but she wasn't afraid. His rage was directed inward. The presence that had invaded him had left him as shaken as she and she knew he wouldn't thank her for noticing that.

"My fault," he whispered, keeping his gaze locked with hers.

"How is *that* your fault?" she demanded and as the fear drained from her body, her own sense of indignation on his behalf flared into life.

"Because the demon should never have been able to enter my thoughts. Should never have been given the opportunity."

"How did it happen then?"

"I…relaxed the mental barriers I usually have in place," he admitted, folding his arms over his broad, muscled chest. "I lost myself in you, and let my guard down." He lifted his chin, threw his hair back from his face and added, "And because of that, I nearly cost you your life."

"You didn't, though. I'm safe and the demon's gone." A single thread of fear still rippled through her as she wondered about the connection she shared with Kieran. As it grew, would the demon's power to reach her grow as well? It was something she would have to think about carefully. Later. When she was alone and sure that Kieran wouldn't be able to hear her thoughts so easily.

"You don't have to fear me," he said tightly and she could hear how it hurt him to have to say it.

"Obviously you're still dipping into my mind whenever you feel like it. I wish you'd stop. It's creepy."

A small, weary smile curved his mouth. "I will try to remember."

"Thanks." In the silence, she wondered if now that she and Kieran had *mated,* would the demon be able to find her more easily in Kieran's presence? Maybe she should make a run for it. She'd gotten out of the castle once, she could to it again. Maybe if she put plenty of distance between herself and Kieran, the demon wouldn't be able to find her. And it sure wouldn't be able to use her to get to Kieran.

"No," he said. "Don't think to run again. You will not succeed a second time."

"You're doing it again."

"Clearly I must," he countered. "You're a very headstrong woman. To keep ahead of your plans, I must know your thoughts."

"Fine," she snapped. "You know what I'm thinking. Tell me I'm wrong, then. We're so close now, Kieran, the demon can find me even more easily if I'm with you. If I left—"

"I would be spending all of my time finding you rather than tracking the demon. Innocents would die."

The air left her lungs like a balloon with a slow leak. That's just how she felt. Deflated.

"If we're together, we're that much easier to find. Why would it look for me if I wasn't with you?"

"To draw me to you, woman," he said and the old snarl was back in his voice. Strangely comforting, somehow. "It won't be able to get into my mind again, I have ways of blocking it. But if you were out there alone, Julie, you would not be safe. You must believe me. Even if you are now frightened of me—you are safe only with me."

"I'm not frightened of you, Kieran." When his eyebrows lifted in silent question, she added, "Okay fine, I'm still a little weirded out, but what happened a few minutes ago? That wasn't you. You wouldn't hurt me. I know that."

He shook his head slowly. "You defend me? After..." He waved one hand at the bed behind her.

She tried a smile and realized that it wasn't as forced as she had expected. "I defend you. And if I can, then there's no reason for you to punish yourself."

He blew out a breath and cautiously closed the distance between them. His hands came down on her shoulders as he looked into her eyes, searching for the fear that was now buried deep inside her.

"I wasn't expecting the demon to link with me," he admitted. "I will be now. It won't happen again."

She nodded, accepting his statement at face value. For the moment, anyway.

"This has never happened to you before?"

"Never," he said tightly, disgust clear on his features. Drawing her back to the bed, he eased her down, then sat beside her. "I told you before, every demon is different. Just as every Guardian is different."

"Explain again," she said, watching him as the play of colored light shifted over his face with his changing expression.

He sighed, lifted his head and stared through the French doors at the night beyond the glass. When he spoke again, his voice was soft, nearly hypnotic.

"The demon dimensions are filled with beings eager to cross into this one, where the prey is easy."

"Prey." She swallowed. "That would be *us*. Humans."

"Yes. Each demon is as different as each mortal is from another. Some have powers others lack. Some are evil, some are…not."

"Not evil demons. Interesting." She nodded. "Go on."

"As there have always been demons, so have the Guardians always existed," he started. "We are immortal unless we *choose* to quit the fight."

"Does that happen often?"

"No," he said with a slow shake of his head. "But after thousands of years, even an Immortal can tire of the never-ending battles."

She didn't like the idea of Kieran walking off into the sunset, and blocked the image from her mind, just in case he was listening in again.

"The oldest remaining of us was once a Centurion in ancient Rome."

"Whoa." Just the thought of a Roman soldier in modern times was enough to really stagger the imagination.

A quick smile touched his mouth and was gone

again in an instant. "There are thousands of us, each with different abilities. We are assigned a territory to protect and rarely leave it."

"Who does the assigning?"

He laughed a bit and said, "You are a reporter, aren't you?"

"Relax, Kieran. This isn't for the papers, it's for *me*."

"I know that. Truly." He touched her hand then pulled back as if half worried she would pull away before he could. "His name is Michael."

"Mike?" Julie just stared at him. "The head Guardian's name is *Mike?* That's so…boring."

"I will be sure to tell him you said so."

"Who is he?"

"I don't believe anyone knows," Kieran mused. "He appears at the moment of death and offers the choice I have told you about." Shifting his gaze around the room, he then turned to look at her. "Once you choose, you are trained, given an endless supply of wealth—"

"Handy," she said, understanding now how this amazing castle had come to be.

"—and you are given assignments."

"How? Letter? Telegram? Phone call?"

"Sometimes," he said, smiling at her incredulous tone. "And sometimes, it is no more than a telepathic message, warning us that a demon has entered our territory."

"Do you ever wish you'd chosen differently?" she asked, reaching to stroke the back of his hand with her fingertip.

He sucked in air and pulled his hand from under hers. "No."

"Why, Kieran? When it was your turn to choose, why didn't you just go on to Heaven or whatever? Why choose to fight for eternity?"

"It is what I know." He shrugged. "What I do."

"Why did that English knight kill you?" she asked quietly. She figured now was the best time to ask the question that had bothered her since she'd first looked into his past. He'd asked her not to discuss the day of his death, but she knew that the guilt he was feeling at the moment, might be enough to prompt him to tell her the story. "When I saw your memories, I knew that he was there only to kill you. Why?"

His mouth flattened into a grim line and he inhaled sharply through gritted teeth. "He was my wife's lover," Kieran said, spitting the words out as if they tasted bitter. "She wanted me dead so she could marry him. Elevate her station at court."

That was the secret behind the old pain in his eyes. Betrayal. Well she sure knew how that felt. But for him, a man of his times, the pain must have been even sharper.

"Bitch."

An unexpected snort of laughter shot from him. "Yes, she was. A shame I didn't discover that fact until *after* I was dead."

"And you've been alone ever since."

He turned his head to look at her. "Until you."

How could a man look so powerful and so haunted at the same time? And how could that combination affect her so deeply? She felt his strength and even, staggeringly enough, an out of character humility. This man's strength and confidence and well, arrogance, was so much a part of him, it shook her to the bone to see him even slightly humbled.

"And you believe I'm your Destined Mate."

"I know it," he said quietly. "As do you."

The duvet slipped down her shoulders and his upper arm brushed hers. Electricity arced between them, white-hot and insistent and though Julie wanted to deny the truth, she simply couldn't.

They'd known each other only a few days and yet he was more a part of her than anyone she'd ever known before. What did that mean? For her future? For her *life?* If she was his Destined Mate, did that mean giving up everything else in her life that was important to her? Her work? Her home? The simple joy of going to a mall and *not* being hunted by a psycho demon?

But his eyes were locked on hers, demanding that she acknowledge what lay between them and she couldn't remain silent.

"Yes," she finally said. "I know it. What I don't know is what it means. For me. For you."

He nodded, clearly pleased that she had at least, accepted the inevitable. "Now that we have mated, it means that I will have the strength I need to capture the demon."

"That's why you brought me here, isn't it?" she said. "Not so much to protect me, but to use me to gain the strength you needed."

"Yes," he answered, the truth shining in his eyes, but melded with another truth he didn't give voice to. "In the beginning, I suspected who you were and wanted the power you could give me."

"And what I wanted didn't matter."

"No," he said, "it didn't." As if he couldn't sit beside her and confess to how he'd used her for his own purposes, he pushed off the bed and stalked naked to the French doors. Once there, he turned to look at her again. "What mattered was being able to track the demon. To fulfill my duty. Julie, I have lived for centuries, doing just that. My only thought to protect those I swore to defend."

She did understand. She *felt* his emotions sliding through him in a tangled web of frustration and pride and…not love, but *need*. And still, she had to ask, "Just where did I fit into your duty, Kieran? Aren't I one of those you're supposed to be protecting? Defending?"

"You are and I have."

"Yet you used me," she pointed out, feeling the sharp sting of it slap her anew.

"I did."

He lifted his chin and God, he looked magnificent. Moonlight shone all around him, bathing him in a silvery glow that looked more like a pulsing aura. His skin gleamed bronze in the pale light and despite the fear still hiding inside her, she wanted him so much she could taste his skin beneath her lips.

"And would again," he added, "if my duty demanded it. I will do what I must to capture this demon."

"Capture? Why not kill it?" Surprised at her sudden, bloodthirsty compulsion, she snapped her mouth shut and waited for his answer.

"Demons are not easy to kill. They are very nearly as immortal as we. The only way to actually *kill* a demon is with 'the blood of the innocent.' And since killing an innocent, even to destroy a demon, is wrong—we capture them." Clearly he didn't like that admission, but it was, apparently, the simple truth. "Guardians hunt them, track them, then return them to their own hell dimension. And the longer this one is free to roam your city killing its people, the stronger it becomes."

"But now you're stronger, too."

"Yes. And I *will* find it."

"Because we've mated."

The hollow sound of her words must have reached him because he walked quickly to her and pulled her to her feet. The duvet dropped to the floor, unnoticed as he looked directly into her eyes.

Kieran felt the jumble in her mind, her thoughts

colliding with each other as she tried to make sense of all he had told her. Admiration filled him. She was truly an amazing woman. Her innate strength and the flexibility of her mind gave her insight into truths that others would never see.

Guilt still choked him, a hard knot of misery lodged in his throat. He had relaxed his guard to better enjoy the melding of his and Julie's minds. To savor the sensation of truly being connected to another living soul.

And she had very nearly paid for his selfishness.

He wouldn't allow the violence of his existence to bleed into her life. Decision made, he paused momentarily to concentrate on the feel of her skin beneath his palms. The soft, silky coolness of her flesh. His gaze dropped, from her full breasts, to her narrow waist and rounded hips and then back to the deep green eyes that called to him, always.

"We *are* Mates, that is true." Kieran moved one hand to cup her cheek and his touch was warm, gentle, as if to make up for what had happened earlier. Knowing that he had frightened her, that he'd touched her with violence was almost more than he could bear. Which made what he was going to say that much more right.

"But know this. When this hunt is finished, when the demon is returned to its hell, I will let you go."

"Let me go?" she repeated. "You mean you'll *allow* me to leave?"

A small, sad smile touched his mouth. "You are not a woman a man *allows* anything. I meant only that I won't try to keep you here. You can return to the life you led before we met."

She blinked, surprised and unsure of just what to say. "What about the Destined Mates thing? *Can* we separate?"

"It has not been done before," he admitted, his hands on her bare shoulders becoming more gentle, more tender. His fingers caressed her skin idly as he thought about what he was suggesting. "Only a very few Guardians have found their Destined Mates through the years, and of those, none that I know of have separated."

"Then—"

"We can each survive without the other," he whispered, though in his mind and heart, he knew that neither of them would ever feel truly complete without the other. But he wouldn't bind her to him with old traditions that meant nothing in this modern age. "This is not the life you chose, Julie

Carpenter. And I will not have you lose what is most important to you because of my duty. So when this is finished, we will part. I will leave Los Angeles. You'll never have to see me again."

She actually swayed on her feet and he read confusion in her eyes. Small of him, but he was pleased that he could read no pleasure in her at the thought of seeing the last of him.

"Stay with me until this is finished. Allow me to protect you and spend my energies where they are most needed," he said, "and when it's done, you're free to go."

"I'll stay. I won't run again." She met his gaze evenly, lifting her chin in a small show of defiance. "But don't keep me in the dark, Kieran. Don't shut me out."

"Agreed," he said and let her go, symbolically and physically, taking a step back from her, before he could give in to his own desire to feel her body beneath his again.

"Good," she said, walking to him, arms outstretched, a flash of hunger in her eyes. "And now, Destined Mate, I need you inside me."

"Are you sure?" he asked, battling the incredible roar of need pounding in his blood. "After…"

"*Especially* after," she said and pressed up close to him. She slid her hands down the length of his body and closed her fingers around the hard, thick proof of his need.

He hissed in a breath as her fingers danced along his length, caressing, stroking, leading the tip of him to rub against her wet heat.

"Woman," he admitted through gritted teeth, "you unman me."

She grinned up at him. "God, I hope not."

Chapter 13

The next few days crawled past.

Tension hung over the castle in a thick blanket and charged the very air with enough pressure that even breathing was nearly painful. Kieran and Nathan spent most of their time in the in-house gym, training loudly enough that Julie could hear the ringing of swords clashing together all through the castle.

Julie tried to stay out of their way, spending most of her time in the castle's extensive library. And, since she couldn't get in touch with the newspaper—Kieran refused to let her tell anyone where she was—she had begun work on that book she used to dream of writing.

But it wasn't easy to concentrate. She couldn't stop thinking about the battle that was inevitably headed their way. The demon was still out there. She couldn't feel it, but she knew it was there.

When Kieran wasn't training, he was out hunting for signs of the demon. Every time he came back from one of these unsuccessful hunts, she felt his frustration like a living, breathing thing in the castle.

Their connection had only strengthened and grown in the last several days. When he came to her room in the middle of the night, their lovemaking was fierce yet tender, as if he were determined to eradicate all of her memories of the night the demon had invaded his mind.

She could have told him that wasn't necessary. But he wouldn't have believed her.

Sitting back in the wide, burgundy leather chair, she tucked her legs up under her, set her unread book down onto her lap and stared out the window at the neatly trimmed garden beyond. Even in January, there were some flowering bushes and the lawn was as tidy and well cared for as a putting green on a first-class golf course.

Everything about this place was as magical as a fairy tale.

Even the dark prince who called it home.

"What are you thinking?"

She turned her head, giving Kieran a forced smile as he walked into the room. "You mean you didn't peek?"

Nodding, he walked toward the bar on one side of the room and lifted a crystal decanter filled with a pale amber liquid. Pouring himself a glass of brandy, he set the crystal down, picked up his glass and took a sip. "I confess, I did. Dark prince?"

She laughed shortly. The man was incorrigible. She no longer remembered what it was like to have her thoughts be her own.

"I can teach you to erect barriers to protect your privacy," he offered, crossing the room to sit down on the heavy cocktail table in front of her.

She watched him and saw the quick spark of sorrow in his eyes before he could hide it from her. "No," she said quietly. "There's no point, is there? When the demon is captured, you're leaving."

He would be gone. She would drive her car up this hill, stare at the castle and know that Kieran wouldn't be coming back. How would she live with knowing she would never see him again? How would she survive without his mind touching hers? Without his hands on her body? Without the sense of him nearby?

The thought of returning to her life, being alone again, was less appealing than it had been at the beginning of all of this. In a few short days, Kieran had become not just a part of her life, but the center of it. Without him, the coming years looked bleak at best.

"I should have had it by now." His grip on the fragile crystal glass tightened until Julie was half surprised it didn't simply shatter. He took a long swallow of the liquor. "It killed another woman last night."

"I know." She tried not to watch the news, but when Kieran was near, she didn't have to. She felt the waves of fury emanating off of him in thick, dark waves that left her as miserable as he was.

"I found its trail," he said, rising to stalk around the wide room with long, quick strides. "Followed it into the hills and then back into the city. From alley to alley, I walked just a step or two behind it. Its energy trace is clear, but its power has grown enough that it loses itself in the rush of the city. Just like Whitechapel, it eludes me and it continues to kill."

"You'll find it."

He stopped short and shot her a hard look. "Not soon enough."

Julie unfolded her legs, stood and walked to him. "I haven't felt it again."

"No. It won't be that foolish again. It won't risk connecting to you, knowing that I would be aware and use that thread of connection to find it."

"Well," she said, wrapping her arms around his middle and burying her head against his chest, "that makes me feel both better and worse."

One of his arms came around her shoulders and he rested his chin on top of her head. Julie sighed, enjoying the contact. Somehow, Kieran had become almost a touchstone for her. The one constant in an ever-changing world where danger lurked around every corner and nothing was as she'd always thought it was.

After a long moment, he said quietly, "I have an appointment I must keep this afternoon. And I'd like you to go with me so I can be sure you're safe."

She tipped her head back. "Leave the castle? Actually go beyond the gate and into the city? You bet."

He smiled sadly. "Staying here has been hard for you."

"A great prison is still a prison, Kieran."

"You are not a prisoner."

She inhaled deeply. "I know. It's just…I'm not used to having to answer to anyone else. I like my independence and having it stripped away is…annoying."

One corner of his mouth twitched. "You bear it well."

"No, I don't." But Julie chuckled and thought how strange it was to find comfort in a man who only a short time ago had thrown her ordinary world into turmoil.

"I warn you," he said, tipping her face up to his, "with both of us out there, in the open, the demon will be tempted to try to end this."

"You mean, kill me."

"I won't allow it." Kieran's arms tightened around her as if he could protect her by simply *willing* it. "You will be safe with me, Julie."

"I'm counting on that," she said, sounding a lot braver than she felt.

"Are you really going?" Nathan's voice came from the open doorway and Julie stepped back from Kieran to face the man openly staring at them.

"I gave my word," Kieran said simply.

"I could take your place."

"No." Kieran set his brandy glass down onto a nearby table and said, "I'm going. And Julie is going with me."

The Navy SEAL was obviously disgusted when he asked, "Don't trust me to keep an eye on her anymore?"

"I said I was sorry," Julie started, for the dozenth time in the last few days. But, as always, Nathan didn't want to hear her apologies. He was, in fact, trying to forget entirely that she had ever escaped his watch.

"It's not a question of that," Kieran said.

"Fine." Nathan shook his head, and slammed his hands onto his hips as his gaze narrowed. "But take it from me, she's slippery."

"I'll bear that in mind."

An appointment Kieran refused to cancel because he'd given his word.

Julie didn't know exactly what she'd been expecting.

A meeting with his attorneys?

A sword fight?

A meeting of Immortals to discuss battle plans?

She never would have expected this. Her gaze locked on Kieran as he sat before a rapt audience of three-year-olds, all listening wide-eyed to his stories of Knights and Ladies. Since the moment they'd entered the Camelot preschool for chronically ill children, Kieran had been drawn away from her and feted by the kids. They clearly adored him and one look at his pale eyes and unusually animated expression let her know the feeling was mutual.

In this place, Kieran was a hero. He had endowed the facility so that sick children would have a safe place to play and learn. So that they wouldn't be teased by healthy children because they had to use crutches, or wheelchairs or oxygen tanks.

Tears stung the backs of Julie's eyes as she watched a little blond boy in a back brace carefully touch the sword Kieran held out to him. The awestruck wonder in that child's eyes was enough to wring a tear from a stone. Clearly Kieran was no stranger to this place. The kids knew him, the parents couldn't thank him often enough and the staff hustled to meet his every wish.

I will be here for a while, Kieran said, his voice whispering through her mind. *I've asked someone to give you a tour of the place before the official ceremony.*

Julie smiled. She would really miss this private chitchatting. As the crowd talked and milled around her, she answered him just as silently. *Don't worry about me. You just enjoy yourself.*

He gave her a brief grin that nearly toppled her with the power behind it, then added, *You're safe here.*

I know.

She felt the absence of tension as physically as she would have in peeling off a sweater on a warm day. Here, there was no threat. Here, there were only kids to entertain and important people to feed.

Today at Camelot—a name which she was sure Kieran had suggested—there was a crowd of people gathered for the ceremonial opening of the hospital wing. At least a hundred or more people milled around, sampling the excellent buffet and drinking expensive champagne.

Parents of the sick kids mingled with doctors and some of the wealthiest movers and shakers in L.A. The only people *not* present, were reporters—and Julie had to smile. It was the one request Kieran had made and those in charge had happily fulfilled it. No one wanted to argue with a man who had personally guaranteed that the facility would never have to worry about fund-raisers.

"He's done a wonderful thing here," Grace Johnson, the woman in charge of Camelot said as she guided Julie away from the crowd and down a long hallway to the new hospital wing for a personal tour. "The children are happy, and their parents don't have to worry about their safety."

"It's amazing," Julie said, filled with pride at what Kieran had done. The dark warrior, solitary, cut off from the world, leading a life of such extreme solitude it would drive most men insane, had cared enough to make life a little easier for sick children.

Was it any wonder she loved him?

Surprise flickered in her mind, then dazzled her completely. Of course she loved him. She'd tried to tell herself it was just lust. Or the fact that they'd been involved in nothing but stressful, dangerous…inherently sexy situations from the moment they'd met.

But it was so much more.

Look what he'd done. The building, complete with conical towers, pennant flags streaming from their tips, was perched on a cliff overlooking the ocean—not far from the Santa Monica pier where she and Kieran had made love for the first time.

The view of the sunset streaking across the horizon was incredible. Crimson and deep orange bled together in the twilight sky, staining the water below with shimmering color that was nearly blinding in its intensity. It was almost magical and she understood completely why the children were so happy here. It was a world apart from the reality of their lives. Here, there was room for imagination and daydreams.

The building was beautifully appointed and even the new hospital wing had a friendly, non-threatening air to it. The walls were a soft blue and decorated with the paintings the children had created. The empty beds were shaped like race cars for the boys and glass slippers for the girls. There were toys and chairs and even the IV poles were painted to look like candy canes. Every tiny detail was perfect, designed to take the fear out of being ill.

Planned to maintain children's sense of self despite their limitations.

"I can't tell you how much the children enjoy Mr. MacIntyre's visits," Grace was saying, strolling proudly down the long, brightly lit hallway.

"Does he come often?"

"Once a month, without fail. Once that man makes a promise, he never breaks it. And he just mesmerizes those kids with stories about knights in shining armor." Grace paused, looked at Julie and shook her head in admiration. "I swear, the man uses such detail in his stories, it's almost as if he lived them."

Julie smiled to herself. "He's an unusual man."

"You can say that again." Grace checked her watch and said, "If you'll excuse me, I want to go back in and make sure that Mr. MacIntyre has everything he needs. The ceremony should start in an hour, so there's no rush to get back in there. You just make yourself comfortable, look around all you want. Any friend of Mr. Mac's is always welcome here."

"Thank you." Julie wandered through the last

few rooms, in no hurry to get back to the crowded main room.

Alone, she moved down the hall, peeked into closed rooms and found the back door that led to a fenced backyard outfitted with playground equipment, sandboxes, tricycles and…a detailed, miniature-castle playhouse, equipped with wheelchair ramps and even a drawbridge.

She laughed aloud at the magic of it and walked to the castle to peek inside. Her heart full, she hugged the newfound knowledge of her love close and tried to imagine how she would ever live without him.

He'd made a vow to let her go—and as even Grace had just reminded her, once Kieran gave his word on something, he didn't go back on it. So whether she loved him or not, he would be walking away from her life as completely as he'd entered it.

The demon is here—

A voice in her mind. *Kieran?*

Run. Take the back exit. Down the steps to the beach. I'll meet you there. Go now.

Oh God. Fear stabbed her through, bubbled up in her throat and nearly strangled her. All of those kids. Their parents. No. Don't think about that, she ordered herself, already heading for the locked gate leading to the beach steps. Kieran would protect the innocents. Just as he would protect her.

She flipped the latch placed high on the gate, rushed through and slammed it closed behind her. The wind caught her hair, threw it across her eyes and she whipped her head back to clear her vision. Waves crashed on the shore, a roaring pulse of sound that beat out a rhythm she followed on the steep, narrow stairs.

Her black leather boots hit each step with a solid thunk of sound that reverberated up her spine. Her fingers curled around the cold iron banister and held on tight. Wouldn't do her any good to escape the demon only to break her neck on her wild flight to the beach.

She chanced a look back up the stairs as she made a sharp curve and worried when she didn't see Kieran right behind her. Was he fighting the demon already? Was there even now a battle going on in front of those children? Was Kieran in danger?

Hurry, Julie!

Grateful to sense that short command in her mind, she hurried her steps, hit the bottom and stepped into the sand, feeling it shift beneath her feet. The sun was almost completely down now and twilight was blending into the coming night. The first stars shone from the clear, black sky and the wind and roar of the ocean slapped at her, as if warning her to go back.

Go back.

"There you are."

She spun on her heel to face the man speaking.

Not Kieran.

He had a neatly trimmed beard and eyes that were as black as the sky overhead. When he smiled, a cold chill shot down Julie's spine.

While he watched her, she heard again, *Run, Julie. Go now.*

"It was you."

"Oh, yes," the demon said affably, stroking one hand across its beard. "And may I say you were easier to reach than I had expected."

"Great," she said, glancing around her, looking for—*anything*. But there were no others on the beach. Up and down the sand, there was emptiness, as if everyone had sensed the presence of evil and had stayed away.

Everyone but her, that is.

"What do you want?" she asked, backing up slowly in the sand that felt as treacherous as mud.

"I should think that would be obvious." It came closer, the demon in a man suit, and gave her another smile that warned her of misery to come. "I want *you* and then the Guardian."

Julie shot a silent message to Kieran, hoping he would hear. *On the beach, Kieran. The demon.*

"Thank you," it said. "Very kind."

"I'm not doing it for you," Julie snapped and wondered even as she did, what the human male had been thinking, to give its life and body over to a demon. "Kieran's going to send your ass back to whatever hell you came from."

The smile faded, the black eyes narrowed and the demon took a quick, heart-stopping step forward. "He will not. The longer I'm free, the stronger I become."

I'm coming.

Relief, thick and sweet, rushed through her veins until she felt the demon's delight.

Maybe she could distract it. Keep it off guard until Kieran got there. "If you're so damn strong, why've you been hiding from him?"

"Not hiding," it assured her with a sigh of pleasure, "amusing myself."

Oh God.

"So many lovely women here," it mused, and inhaled sharply, deeply. "It is good to be here among you again. You have progressed much in the last hundred years or so, but thankfully, there are still those among you willing to hand over their bodies to me."

"How did you get him?" she asked, running her gaze up and down the rather ordinary-looking man who now housed a vicious demon.

"This one?" It smiled. "This one was eager for me. Bob Robison possessed the potential for great evil. He simply had no direction. Until I—" it swept her a mocking bow "—came along. Since then, we have gotten along admirably."

A demon named Bob.

Why that struck her as funny, Julie couldn't have said. Probably hysteria. And who could blame her?

"Why?" she asked, stalling, keep stalling, get it to talk, make time for Kieran to reach her. "Why kill all of those women? Alicia? Why hurt Kate?"

"Ah, your little friends," it said, mouth curving into a smile of reminiscence. "I don't mind talking, you know. It's always pleasant to share one's proud deeds with a truly interested audience."

"Great." She swallowed hard and fought against a rising tide of sickness lurching in her stomach.

"And besides, we're in no hurry. I'm content to await your Guardian before killing you."

"Thanks," she muttered, sending another wild thought into the mists—*Kieran!*

"Your friend was delicious," the demon purred, licking its lips as if remembering a particularly juicy meal. "She whimpered and pleaded for her life. Music."

Rage crowded against the fear crawling through her and Julie glared at him.

"Ah!" It smiled, pleased at her attitude. "If only she had had more of *your* vinegar. It would have been more gratifying. As for your other friend…" The demon paused, and frowned thoughtfully. "Clearly I should have taken more time with her. But once I've dispensed with your Guardian— and you, my dear—perhaps I'll just pay her a return visit and give her my full attention."

"You stay the hell away from Kate," Julie said grimly.

It laughed. "You really are a delight. So fiery and full of spirit. It's no wonder the Guardian has become enamored of you."

Julie took a staggering step backward as her boot heel came down on a rock. "You bastard, Kieran's going to turn you inside out."

"Brilliant," it shouted, laughing again with a shriek of sound that was nearly ear shattering. "You entertain me so."

"Julie!" Kieran's shout sounded out loud over the roar of the ocean and the wail of the wind.

She turned, looked up and saw him standing at the top of the cliff staring down at them. She didn't need to see his eyes to feel the fury emanating from him like thick ripples in the air.

Glancing at the demon she said, "You're about to be entertained in a whole new way, you son of a bitch."

Ignoring her now in favor of the man it had been waiting for, the demon moved suddenly, wrapping one arm around Julie's neck, hauling her back against it.

"Guardian!" it shouted. "Come and play and maybe your woman will survive the night!"

Julie tore at the demon's arm, slicing its skin with her nails, pulling and tugging with all her strength and yet, she might as well have been trying to push a mountain out of her way. The demon's strength was awesome and for the first time, she really feared for Kieran's safety.

Yes, he was strong. And fast. And trained.

And immortal.

But he could be hurt. He could be wounded badly. He'd told her of Guardians who had been nearly destroyed protecting the innocent.

As the demon's own fury wrapped itself around her like the coils of a hungry python, panic reared up inside her. The demon was going to kill her and she hadn't even had the chance to tell Kieran how much she loved him.

In a heartbeat of time, she experienced the sorrow of knowing that no matter what happened here, her time with Kieran was almost over. If she died, he wouldn't know of her love. And if she lived, she would still lose him to his own sense of honor.

"Kieran, *no!*" She shouted the warning, knowing it was useless. Knowing he would ignore her.

Knowing that nothing would keep him from her side.

He wouldn't turn away from the battle he'd been trained for. Wouldn't turn away from his duty. Or her.

And in the next instant, he proved her right.

He jumped off the edge of the cliff. The sides

of his coat billowed out around him, looking like wings as he sailed through the air, sword held high, pale eyes murderous.

Chapter 14

He landed lightly on his feet, then immediately sprang up, sword at the ready and a part of Julie was flabbergasted despite her fear.

"Cease," Kieran announced, not looking at Julie at all, instead spearing the demon's gaze with determination. "Let the woman go and we will settle this."

Julie felt the rush of adrenaline pumping through the demon as it tightened its hold on her throat. Her breath was cut off and her vision began to swim, blurring as her lungs fought for air. She looked at Kieran and even though she was sure this was her last moment, she couldn't help feeling a thrill of pride and admiration in him.

He looked impossibly tall, fearless. His black hair twisted in the wind, his pale, icy eyes were narrowed in tightly leashed fury and his very body hummed with the power just waiting to be turned loose on the demon. In the dim light of the stars, Kieran looked like an age-old avenger and she wondered why the demon wasn't shaking in its sneakers.

"The woman matters to you, yes?" the demon taunted.

Julie groaned, still tugging ineffectually at the arm snaking around her throat.

"Matters enough that should you kill her, I will not only send you to hell, I will follow you there," Kieran vowed, his voice soft and deadly. "And I will spend eternity making you pay."

"Interesting," the demon mused, stepping to one side and dragging Julie along with him as he moved. Keeping his gaze locked on Kieran, he said, "She doesn't seem very special."

"Let her go," Kieran said, now moving in the same circle the demon had begun. He lifted his sword and starlight glittered magically on the deadly sharp blade. "This battle is ours. As it has always been."

"You stopped me once," the demon said and relaxed its grip on Julie long enough for her to gulp a breath of air. "I won't be stopped again."

"Your time here is over," Kieran said and sliced his blade through the air, making it whistle with promise, purpose.

Julie stumbled and the demon shoved her, keeping a tight grip on her nonetheless.

"I am eternal," the demon crowed, lifting its head, its black eyes staring at the heavens in defiance before shifting that gaze to Kieran again. "I command legions in hell and I bow to no Guardian."

Kieran dipped and swayed, twisting his sword back and forth in a hypnotic dance as his gaze locked on his opponent. "Your legions mean nothing, demon. Here, there is only you. And me. The woman is no part of this."

It laughed, loud and long and the evil slide of it seemed to thicken the air and give it a bitter, horrific feel. "There will be time enough for her later." It dragged one hand across her cheek and Julie shuddered. "I will take her at my leisure and you will know, Guardian, that she paid for your insolence."

"Will you continue to talk, demon?" Kieran demanded with a sneer of contempt, "Or will you fight?"

"Let it end, then."

The demon tossed Julie away from it and she landed hard on the sand, rolling several feet from the two men squaring off against each other.

As if summoned by the gathering of power on the beach, clouds scuttled in from the horizon, hurtling across the sky, blocking out the moon and the stars. The threatening clouds crashed into each other in claps of thunder that rattled every bone in Julie's body. Lightning flashed and struck the sand not twenty feet away and she felt the deadly rush of heat swamp her bones.

Neither the Guardian nor the demon so much as flinched.

The wind howled, screaming past the three of them, tearing at clothes, plucking at their hair, tossing grains of sand into the air and hurling them like tiny bullets to rip and tear at eyes and skin. Waves rose, defying the outgoing tide to roar and smash into shore, lifting a showering spray into the electrified air.

Julie couldn't tear her gaze from the two combatants. As she watched, the demon lifted one hand and seemed to tear a sword from the very air. Thunder rolled, lightning flashed and two swords came together in a clash of sound that was deafening.

Kieran swooped across the sand, wind tearing at his coat, his hair a flying black halo around his head. His jaw was clenched and his two-fisted grip on the hilt of his sword was so tight that Julie could see the whitening of his knuckles.

She braced herself on the heated sand and watched breathlessly, caught in the web of power emanating from the two fighting an age-old battle.

The demon laughed, a wild, terrifying sound that lifted into the air and screamed through Julie's bloodstream. She squinted against the flying sand, lifted one arm to protect her eyes as best she could and held her breath as the demon charged, swinging its sword in a wide arc that had Kieran leaping back to avoid the blow.

"It is *my* time, Guardian," it howled, spinning in place, lifting its sword as if to pluck the very lightning from the sky. "My time to rule here on this plane of existence. The humans belong to me and my brethren. The time of the Guardian is done!"

Kieran lunged, spearing the tip of his blade

through the demon's side and its shriek of pain was satisfying, if brief. Instantly the demon retaliated, leaping into the air, jumping *over* Kieran to land behind him and slice its own blade into the Guardian's shoulder.

Julie screamed as Kieran staggered and another flash of lightning shot from the sky and singed the air. Her heart in her throat, she went up on all fours, fingers clawing into the sand as if holding on to the world.

Kieran felt her fear. He couldn't risk looking at her, though. Couldn't distract himself by worrying about her. When he'd first heard her calling him from the beach, he'd felt raw panic unlike anything he'd felt in centuries. Knowing that the demon had her, could kill her, end her, at any moment had nearly paralyzed him.

He'd escaped the school by bending everyone's perception of him. Making himself invisible, he'd rushed to the cliffs and looked down on his worst nightmare. Julie in the hands of the demon he was sworn to fight.

To find her alive filled him with more joy than he'd ever experienced before. But to keep her alive, he had to focus on his duty. On the one thing he did better than anyone else on the face of the planet.

Julie's thoughts flashed through his mind like the lightning bolts crashing all around them. Her fear. Her worry.

For *him*.

And his power sang through his blood.

The demon's strength had grown far beyond what it had been back in Whitechapel so long ago. Its might now rivaled Kieran's own and he knew that this fight would be the hardest fought and the most important one of his long, lonely life. He *must* win.

To save Julie.

The demon's blade swung out and Kieran parried it, darting to one side, pulling the demon farther from the woman who crouched on the sand, eyes wide, brain racing.

"I will cripple you," the demon sneered, lunging again, dipping beneath Kieran's blade to take a lethal swipe that only just missed. "And as you lie on the sand, helpless, you will hear me take her. Use her. And as she dies, her screams will echo within you for centuries, Guardian. That, and the knowledge that you failed her."

His blade lifted, Kieran made a stab at the demon again that only just missed and in a heartbeat of time, the demon slipped toward Julie, swinging its sword high.

Kieran's fury nearly blinded him. To capture the demon, he must first incapacitate it. That meant wounding the human body it inhabited. Only then could he use the Guardian netting he carried in his coat pocket. Once captured, the demon would be helpless and easily transported back to its hell.

But he'd never had to fight while trying to protect a human at the same time. Especially not a human he *loved*.

Kieran took one long leap toward the demon, sword outstretched to impale it—but the demon had anticipated him. Ducking low, the demon swung its own blade, deflecting Kieran's blow and landing one itself.

"Kieran!" Julie's scream cut through the tumult of the storm and sliced into him more fully than the sword had done.

Tumbling to the sand, Kieran gathered his strength to attack again and opened his eyes to see her charging the demon like a madwoman, a rock clutched in her fist. *No, Julie. Stay back!* His mind reached for her, but she was beyond hearing.

Her eyes flashed, her features were tight with rage and fear and when she closed on the beast, it lifted its sword…and impaled her.

"Julie!" Kieran's voice lifted into the wind, wild grief drawing her name into a cry of agony that tore through the heavens.

Stunned surprise filled her, dulling the pain until it became no more than a shadow in her mind. Julie felt the blade piercing her through and knew that she should be in agony, but somehow, there was nothing. She felt Kieran's grief stronger than her own pain. She stared into the blackness of the demon's eyes as it laughed down at her and knew it was over.

She'd lost. Everything.

She couldn't move. She could only hang, pinned on the demon's sword, sliding inexorably toward the jeweled, golden hilt. It laughed at her, enjoying her sorrow, thrilling to the end of her dreams, her love, her life.

She heard Kieran as if from a distance and wanted to say so much to him. She wanted to tell

him how she loved him. How she didn't care that
he was an Immortal. Didn't care about the worlds
of differences separating them. She wanted...so
much.

Still dazed, she fell forward, landing against the
demon's chest in a macabre parody of an embrace.
Her hands weakly on its chest, she felt its laughter shudder through her and she winced as it
screamed in victory.

"Guardian I have taken your woman. Now
you will live for centuries, knowing that it was
I who beat you!"

The world spun and began to fade. Julie
watched her blood dripping from her body to pour
over the demon's chest and spatter in weird
patterns on the sand at her feet.

Each breath became an event.

Each heartbeat a victory.

And then the demon's cry of triumph became
something else. She sensed the change as much as
heard it, as the demon screamed, sending its eerie,
high-pitched voice into the night to be swallowed
by the black.

Pushing her from it, the demon staggered back
and Julie lay insensible on the sand. Absently she

watched as it glared at her, confusion and desperation racing through it as it tried to understand what was happening even while it clawed desperately at the river of her blood still raining down its body.

The dark stains crept over its flesh, sliding, spilling, moving as if alive. The demon cried again, screaming in anguish as its skin began to bubble and steam. Fury, frustration, disbelief, each emotion chased the next across its features as it dropped to the sand and writhed, limbs twitching in spasmodic jerks.

Kieran clutched the wound at his side and ran to Julie. His gaze locked on the beast, he watched, spellbound at something he'd never seen in more than four centuries of life.

The demon was dying.

Gathering Julie up in his arms, Kieran cradled her against his chest as if he could somehow stanch the flow of her blood if he just held her tightly enough. And while he held her, the demon shrieked one last furious call, then flashed into fire and disappeared.

At once, the storm around them quieted, the sea calmed, the water lazily stroked the shore with lacy fingers, the wind died into a sighing breeze and the lightning shattered itself behind the clouds.

"Julie," he whispered, smoothing her hair back from her face. So pale. Her skin shone like fine porcelain in the dim shadows cast by the subtle shafts of lightning.

"Don't go," he said, cupping her cheek in his palm, tipping her head back. His heart ached, his battered soul wept. "Please don't go."

"Kieran."

"Yes. God, yes. Julie. Stay with me." Frantic now, he covered the wound in her chest with one hand and felt her life's blood pour from her in an ever-slowing stream.

For the first time in his long, long life, Kieran felt helpless. His strength, his power, his prowess with a blade meant nothing as he knelt in the sand and watched the woman he loved slowly die.

"Have to tell you," she whispered, and her voice was hardly more than a sigh of sound that slipped into his soul and settled there. "Love you, Kieran. Always."

His heart shattered in his chest and agony like nothing he'd ever known welled up inside him. He was loved and he was losing her and there was nothing he could do to stop it.

"I love you," he said and dipped his head to take one sweet kiss. To feel her mouth beneath his one more time. To know the brush of her breath on his skin.

He stared into her eyes and in a rush of knowledge, ancient words came to his mind unbidden. Taking her hand in his, he felt the power of those words slam into him and the need to say them to her was overwhelming.

When he spoke, his voice was no more than a whisper of sound, softer than the wind, more powerful than the sea. "Destined Mates, through time, through eternity. Bound together by ties no man can break. Two bodies, one heart. I claim you and offer you all I am."

She smiled and then sighed her last breath.

Clutching her to him, burying his face in the curve of her neck, he lost himself in the warmth still clinging to her skin, the scent of her faint, floral perfume and the silky feel of her hair.

Emptiness yawned inside him, swallowing his heart, his soul, leaving him a hollowed-out shell of a man. And in his mind, the centuries stretched out before him like eternal torment. He tightened his grip on Julie and holding her close, leaned his head back and shouted at the heavens.

"Damn you, bring her back!" As his fury mounted, the storm began to churn again in response to the earthshaking power rattling from him. But Kieran was past caring. The demon was dead— but so was Julie and *someone* was going to pay. Staggering to his feet, Kieran held her body in his arms and screamed his rage at the Fates who would give him his Mate and then take her from him.

"Michael, hear me!" he shouted, his voice raw with the agony stabbing at him. "Restore her. She wasn't a part of this!"

Thunder crashed overhead, lightning arced in white-hot bolts that stabbed the sand in a wide circle around him, but Kieran stood his ground, a warrior ready to battle whatever he had to. All he cared about…all he'd ever loved in four long centuries, was dead in his arms.

Dropping to his knees, Kieran gave in to the pain racking his soul, bent his head to Julie's and felt hot tears pour from him in a flood of emotions that had been dammed up for far too long.

When another bolt of lightning appeared right beside him, Kieran didn't even look up. "She's dead, damn you," he muttered to the man who stood close.

"I know," Michael said and went down on one knee beside his old friend. He glanced across the sand to the blackened spot where the demon had been destroyed. "The demon's dead. She killed it. 'Blood of the innocent.' Her freely given gift of selflessness has banished the evil. This time permanently."

Kieran lifted his head and glared at the tall, dark-haired man he'd known so well for so long. "Do you think I give a damn about the demon?" He shifted his gaze back to the woman lying so lifeless in his arms and stroked one hand along the line of her jaw. "I care only for her. Restore her, Michael. This wasn't her fight. I won't let her die."

"And if it's her fate to die?" Michael asked.

"The hell with Fate," he shot back, snapping a glare at the other man. "You brought me back from the dead. Do the same for her."

Michael studied him for a long, thoughtful moment, then reached out with one hand and touched Julie's cheek. Instantly her eyes fluttered, opened, and she smiled. "Kieran?"

He grinned and felt his cold, dead heart jump to life again. "Julie. Thank God. How do you feel?"

"Strange," she admitted and clumsily pushed out of his arms, looking around her as though trying to figure out where she was and how she'd gotten there.

Kieran's arms felt empty without her, but he fisted his hands to keep from grabbing her again. Whatever happened next, he wouldn't interfere. He wouldn't try to make her stay with him. He would let her go if that was the price for her life. At least he would know that she lived.

Silently he stood, then held out one hand to help her to her feet.

She looked at the man beside him and asked, "Who are you?"

"I'm Michael."

She shot a quick look at Kieran. *"Michael?"*

"Yes," he said and couldn't take his gaze off of her. Blood stained her dark blue sweater and shone in the pale wash of golden light that seemed to always surround Michael.

"I don't understand," Julie said, worry glittering in her eyes. "What happened? Kieran—the demon?"

"Dead."

"Dead? How?" She pushed her hair back out of her eyes and looked from one man to the other, obviously confused.

"What do you remember?" Michael asked.

"The fight," she said instantly, biting at her lower lip and furrowing her brow as she tried to make sense of too many things at once. "The demon, it stabbed Kieran and I was so furious, I grabbed a rock and—" She stopped, stared at Kieran and said, "It stabbed me. I fell and you were there and you kissed me and I...*died*." She staggered back a step or two, wrapped her arms around her middle and whispered, "Oh God, I remember dying. The whole bright light thing and everything." Her gaze snapped up. "What the *hell* is going on?"

Before Kieran could speak, Michael silenced him with a look. "You killed the demon with a selfless sacrifice," he said and his voice was almost like a song, perfect and slow and beautiful. "And now, there are choices to be made."

"Choices?" Kieran's gruff voice interrupted and he took a step toward the other man as if readying to do battle again. "The choice is made. She lives. And she will continue to live."

Michael held up one hand and swept his dark gaze from Kieran to Julie and back again. "No one saw this coming," he admitted with a shrug. "We didn't know that you were Destined Mates—or that Julie would sacrifice herself for you, Kieran."

"We?" Julie asked pointedly.

Michael ignored her. "As Destined Mates, though, you must be allowed to remain together. The question is…*how?*" Drawing a deep breath, the big man continued slowly. "Kieran can choose to leave immortality and the never ending struggle against the darkness behind and become human. To live a mortal life with you, Julie." He paused a moment to let those words sink in before adding, "Or…you can choose to become a Guardian. An Immortal."

Silence dropped over the three of them until Michael spoke up again. "The choice is yours, but you must decide quickly."

Kieran ignored his old friend, stalked across the space separating him from Julie, grabbed her arm and walked her a few steps farther away. Cupping her face in his palms, he stared into her eyes and smiled, really smiled for what felt like the first time ever.

"I will make the choice, Julie," he whispered. "I'll become a mortal. I don't need this life. All I need is *you*. If you will have me."

Julie reached up and covered his hands with her own, drawing in one tentative breath as if testing to see if she really was alive again. But she was. He felt warm and solid and wonderful. She remembered the words he'd spoken to her as she lay dying and they echoed inside her with a power she couldn't deny, even if she'd wanted to. Which she didn't.

"Kieran, I know you love what you do—"

He opened his mouth to speak, but she placed her fingers on his lips to keep him quiet. "And what you do is too important for you to walk away from."

"No," he argued, kissing her fingertips. "Nothing is more important than you."

"Thank you." She smiled and asked quietly, "But, if I were to become an Immortal, could we get married? A real wedding, with guests and my family and everything?"

"Of course."

"Could we have children?"

That beautiful smile faded a little as he shook his head. "No, immortals cannot have children. You would be surrendering your right to ever have your own family."

She took his hands tightly in hers as understanding dawned. "That's why you give so much to children's causes, isn't it? Why you so enjoy spending time with kids."

He nodded and leaned in to kiss her forehead. "We could have that, Julie. Share in the world's children. Even adopt if we wanted to. Other Immortals have."

Swallowing hard, she sadly let go of the dream of her own children and opened herself up to other possibilities. Then she asked, "Can I maintain contact with my family?"

"Certainly," he said, his thumbs stroking her temples. "For a while, anyway. Eventually you would have to settle for phone calls and e-mail, since you would not age and they will."

Never to grow old. How strange that seemed. "And I would have you?"

"Always," he said, his voice a sigh of want and need and love. "For the first time in my too-long life, I know what love is. It is you, Julie Carpenter. *You* are my heart. My soul. My life. And I will love you, eternally."

"And I will love you just as long, Kieran Mac-Intyre." Taking a breath, she gave him back the words he'd given her just before she died. "Destined Mate. Two bodies, one heart."

Finally the decision was so easy. To live forever in love with Kieran? How could she possibly turn that down?

Together, they turned to face Michael and his wide smile let them know how pleased he was by their choice. Stepping forward, he laid one hand on Julie's forehead and she stood still as a flood of warmth and strength and power rushed through her body, tingling every nerve ending, filling every vein.

The wind felt stronger, the roar of the ocean somehow purer and the light shimmering around Michael was so beautiful her eyes ached with it. Every sense she possessed was heightened as she took her first deep breath as an Immortal.

"Welcome to the ranks of the Guardians, Julie Carpenter," Michael said as he stepped back from them. "See that your Mate trains you well."

And in a blinding flash of white-hot light, he was gone.

The storm slowly blew out over the ocean, clouds dissipating to allow the moonlight to stream down onto the beach, illuminating Julie and Kieran in a pale glow that felt like a blessing.

Leaning into the man she loved, Julie wrapped her arms around his middle and turned her head to look up the cliffs at the school they'd left what felt like a lifetime ago. "I suppose you'd better get back in there and finish entertaining the kids."

He held her tightly to him, then turned her face up to his for a long, soul-binding kiss. "I think the children have had enough storytelling for one evening."

"But we can't just disappear. What will everyone think?"

"They will think that the eccentric and reclusive Kieran MacIntyre wanted some time alone with the woman who stole his heart."

"Oh," she said and smiled up at him. "In that case…" She looked around them at the empty beach and the miles of sand stretching out on both sides of them. "Now that I'm a Guardian, too, does that mean I can make myself hidden, too?"

"It does," he said and his eyes flashed as he picked up on her intentions.

"Then why don't we take advantage of that little trick right now?"

"Woman, you will be the death of me," he said, smiling as he followed her into the moonlit darkness.

"Don't worry, love," she said as she stepped into his arms and lifted her face for his kiss. "We're Immortals."

* * * * *

FREE!

4 Books
and a surprise gift!

We would like to take this opportunity to thank you for reading this Mills & Boon® book by offering you the chance to take FOUR more specially selected titles from the Intrigue series absolutely FREE! We're also making this offer to introduce you to the benefits of the Mills & Boon® Reader Service™—

- ★ **FREE home delivery**
- ★ **FREE gifts and competitions**
- ★ **FREE monthly Newsletter**
- ★ **Exclusive Reader Service offers**
- ★ **Books available before they're in the shops**

Accepting these FREE books and gift places you under no obligation to buy, you may cancel at any time, even after receiving your free shipment. Simply complete your details below and return the entire page to the address below. You don't even need a stamp!

YES! Please send me 4 free Intrigue books and a surprise gift. I understand that unless you hear from me, I will receive 6 superb new titles every month for just £3.15 each, postage and packing free. I am under no obligation to purchase any books and may cancel my subscription at any time. The free books and gift will be mine to keep in any case.

18ZEF

Ms/Mrs/Miss/Mr ....Initials ....
BLOCK CAPITALS PLEASE

Surname ....

Address..

....

....Postcode ....

Send this whole page to:
UK: FREEPOST CN81, Croydon, CR9 3WZ